The Firelink Chronicles

Book One

Firelink

By Sandra DiMartino

Shirley,
   Thank you so
much for teaching
me how to journey
to past lives. I
hope you enjoy this
one. XO Sandy

This book is dedicated to

Paul Lowell

You are as much a part of this
Adventure as any of us.
I hope you enjoy revisiting
A time we remembered together.

and to

Mom and Dad

You've always supported and
Encouraged my creativity.
I can't imagine my world any other way,
Nor would I want to.
Thank you so much for that gift
As well as all of the others.

Special Thanks to...

There are so many people along the way who help us on our path. Some of the people who have helped me and whom I would like to thank are: All of the many friends who read <u>Firelink</u> and offered helpful suggestions; Mom for her assistance editing the final proof; Laurie Perkins for sharing her insights; Michele Ferro for her great cover design; Steve Bogart for encouraging me and reminding me not to give up; Roy Bauer for opening the doors that allowed me to meet Taryn and Julia; Shirley Pratt for taking me on my first journey to the past; Tom Cowan for introducing me to the Celtic Way; Frank, Lynn, Michele, Paul, and other deeply loved allies for being fellow travelers and the best support team; my students at Lexington High for reminding me every day how much fun it is to create and to laugh; and, most of all, Taryn, Julia, and all who populate their world. Thank you so much for sharing. My world is far richer because of you.

Chapter One

A sharp pain pierced Taryn's left shoulder a moment after he heard the swish of air behind him. He cursed silently, evaded the full impact of the sword, and turned to face his opponent. Before him was nothing but empty space.

Taryn spun around in confusion. Clearly someone had been here, as there was a tear in his tunic and a shallow wound on his shoulder as testimony to the presence. Bewildered he took another sweep of his surroundings, and it was only then that he spotted a figure in dark clothing slinking into the swamp at the edge of the battlefield.

'Run you coward,' Taryn thought. 'Run while you can. Perhaps someday you and I will meet again. I hope then you'll have the courage to face me.'

All around him the battle raged on, full of men who did have the courage to fight for what they wanted. The British were fighting to expand their territory into Scottish turf, and Taryn and his men were just as determined to prevent that.

Even as he absentmindedly rubbed the wound on his shoulder and wondered about this seemingly random attack, his eyes were sweeping the field. His attention was caught by a small group of British soldiers jockeying into place to surround and cut off a few of his officers. He called to his first officer Gern, and the two of them swiftly moved to thwart the enemy.

~~~~~~~~~~~~~~~~

It was a few hours later when the battle cries had left the field that Taryn was finally able to examine the wound. He was in his tent with his tunic off and his healing supplies laid out on the ground before him. The wound, which was shallow and should have been more nuisance than anything else, was throbbing and oozing. He was just debating the best course of action when the tent flap was thrust aside and his extremely large first officer appeared in the opening. He stopped short when he saw Taryn's wound.

"Damn it Taryn. Why didn't you tell me you'd been hurt?" The concerned look on Gern's face softened his harsh tone.

"Because it's only a scratch, Gern, and I knew you'd make a fuss."

Gern moved closer and glared at the wound on Taryn's shoulder. "It's a very ugly scratch, if you ask me."

"I was just noticing that myself. And I have to admit that it's throbbing a damn sight more that it should be for such a shallow wound." Taryn rubbed his finger over the wound and sniffed. He held his finger out to Gern. "What do you smell?"

Gern looked at him as if he were crazy. "You want me to smell it?"

Taryn smiled at Gern's obvious discomfort. "Yes, I do." He paused and squinted his eyes. "Are you refusing a request from your commanding officer, Gern?"

Gern, who knew that his commanding officer wasn't really threatening him, grunted and leaned closer to the finger and sniffed. Suddenly his bemused expression was replaced by one of concern. "There **is** a strange odor. Far beyond your usual one."

Taryn arched an eyebrow. "Although I appreciate your sense of humor Gern, I wish you would be more specific."

"Sort of like..." Gern paused as he searched his memory, "cloves."

Taryn nodded. "That's what I thought, too."

"Why would someone have cloves on his sword?"

"Because, my friend, the smell of cloves is strong enough to mask the smell of ..."

"Poison." Gern caught on and spoke the word simultaneously with Taryn. "I'll be damned. You've been poisoned, Taryn."

Taryn's expression was wry. "It would appear that way."

"Well, what are we going to do about it?"

"I was just about to figure that out when you barged in." He glanced at his first mate and closest friend out here on the battleground. "Maybe you can help if you're willing."

"Anything, Taryn."

Taryn arched his eyebrow. "You may regret speaking those words when you hear what I have to say." Taryn paused for a moment. "The best course of action is to suck the poison out."

"Well do it then."

"As you can see, it's high on the side of my shoulder – too high for me to reach." He looked at Gern meaningfully.

Gern paled as he realized what was required of him. "Good God. You want me to suck the poison from your shoulder?"

"I do. But be sure not to swallow any of it as it could cause just as much damage to you."

Gern winced. "The things a man has to do for a superior officer." He sighed. "Well, let's be quick about it then. I can't have you losing your arm because of me."

Taryn looked for the powders he would need to neutralize any remaining toxins and to seal the cut. While he was determining the best possible combination, he sent Gern outside to sterilize his dagger in the campfire.

When Gern returned, the two men set out to complete the task quickly and efficiently. Gern sliced a shallow cut in Taryn's shoulder both above and below the wound and sucked out the poison, which he spat on the floor of the tent. Taryn then placed a powder over the wound. The stinging was intense for only a short while, and it was a mere flicker of his eyes that indicated any discomfort whatsoever. After the powder, Gern used the reheated dagger to sear the wound shut. Then he covered it with a cooling salve and clean dressings. When both men were satisfied with the work, Taryn donned a new tunic.

"Thank you, Gern. That was incredibly helpful."

"Don't mention it. Ever." Gern glared at him and laid emphasis on his final words. "**To anyone.**"

Taryn laughed. "Done."

"I don't think I could live it down."

Taryn's eyes twinkled as he thought about the teasing Gern would undergo if word of his skill at sucking wounds were to spread around the camp. "I am definitely seeing some possibilities for future blackmail."

Gern growled and cuffed him lightly on his good shoulder.

Taryn smiled and turned to the powders still on the ground before him. "I'm going to mix an elixir for you to drink."

"Why?"

"Just in case you accidentally swallowed any of the poison."

"I didn't."

"Still, I'd rather be safe."

"The only thing I'm planning to drink right now is a pint of ale. Rumor has it there will be an officer's card game later this evening and I want to be prepared." Gern hesitated. "Were you planning to tell the men about this poison? Perhaps we should warn them that even a minor wound could become serious."

Taryn tipped his head in acknowledgement. "I've been thinking about that. I'm fairly certain this was an experiment this afternoon." He proceeded to tell Gern about the strange events that had occurred earlier. "Something is definitely brewing. Until we know more of what it is they're up to, let's share it only with the officers."

"Maybe you're right. There's no use alarming everyone if this is a one-time occurrence."

"And you'll quickly see that I'm fine. I don't want the men worrying about me. It could affect morale."

"All right. Let me know if you need me. I'll check in later this evening."

"Fine. I'm going to survey the field. How many did we lose?"

"Less than ten this time, and fifteen injuries – none too severe and nothing like yours."

"Have we had a chance to treat the wounded and bury the dead?"

"Being done as we speak."

"Good. Please see that I receive the names of those we've lost. I'd like to write to their families and be sure that they're taken care of when I return home. And I also want to give the list to Julia."

"When you do, be sure to hide that injury from your sister. There'll be hell to pay if she finds out." Gern grunted and left the tent.

"That's for sure," Taryn muttered. If only Gern knew how hard it was to keep anything from his sister. She was uncanny in her ability to ferret out the truth when it came to him. The best he could hope for was to minimize his latest injury with Julia, and in order to do that, he needed to do everything in his power to speed his recovery.

Taryn wished he were as confident as he had sounded with Gern about the poison being completely out of his system. Due to the battle, it had been several hours before he could treat his wound, and there had been plenty of time for the poison to fully enter his bloodstream. In order to be completely sure that he was safe, he needed more specific information about the ingredients in the potion that had been on that sword. And he knew exactly who could help him with that.

He reached out with his mind to communicate with the Hawk. When she heard and answered his call, he quickly filled her in and sent her on a mission.

Chapter Two

Julia had been picking some flowers and herbs in the forest near the castle when thoughts of her brother first came into her mind. Over the past few hours, these thoughts had become more persistent, and she finally had to admit to herself that something was happening with Taryn. Now it was time to determine exactly what that was so that she would know what action to take.

Taryn and Julia had been strongly connected since his birth which had followed hers by sixteen months. As they matured into young adults and studied the arts of healing and enchantment, their bond had become even stronger. It was not unusual for them to be aware of each other's thoughts or activities, especially when one or the other was in a highly charged situation. Since Taryn had left with the army, Julia had been ever vigilant about checking in on her brother and assuring herself of his well-being.

Julia spotted a large, flat rock in a quiet part of the forest where she could sit and concentrate. She slowed her breathing and mentally called to her animal allies to secure the area. When both the Wolf and the Rook appeared in her mind, she asked them to keep a watch out while she checked on Taryn.

Then Julia went more deeply into her trance and focused on her brother. When she had a clear image of him in her mind, she scanned the energy surrounding his body. Something was definitely off, but it didn't seem life threatening. She could sense a dark area near his left shoulder or upper arm. It didn't seem overly concerning, but Julia decided to do some work anyway.

The first thing she did was to pull away the dark area with her hands. Once she was certain that she had removed what she could, she smoothed his energy and pictured white light all around his upper arm. Finally, she surrounded her brother's entire body in a protective golden glow.

When Julia was satisfied that her work was complete, she tapped into the minds of her allies, thanked them for their help, and released their energy. She opened her eyes to see the late afternoon sun shining through the trees in the forest. As she hurried to gather her basket of herbs and flowers and head back to the castle, Julia was aware that there was still a great deal of work she had to do before her nightly communication with her brother.

Her primary mission this evening was to be sure that everything was in place for tomorrow's journey. As Julia approached the walls of the castle grounds, she veered off the main road and headed for a little-known, hidden access point to the stables, and past them to the castle itself. It was a tunnel which Julia and Taryn had discovered and used as children whenever they wanted to sneak into or out of the castle grounds without alerting the guards.

As she walked through the tunnel to the stable, she reviewed her plans for the upcoming day. Satisfied that she had foreseen every possible issue, she set about making her final checks for the evening.

When Julia reached the stables, she quickly located the stable boy who had often helped her out in the past and was about to help her out once more.

"Stephen, is everything ready for tomorrow?"

"Yes, m'lady."

"It's imperative that the horses are rested, saddled, and waiting at the appointed hour."

"They will be."

"And the supplies?"

"Packed in the carriage under the floorboards."

"Good. It must seem as if Thomas and I are merely going on a short ride around the grounds."

"It will."

"And if asked, all you know about Nanny is that she's going to visit a dear friend in the countryside. It'll be safest that way."

"You can count on me."

Julia smiled at the very serious twelve-year-old before her. "I know that, Stephen." She leaned down and gave him a quick peck on the cheek and a few coins. "Thank you, again. You are most trustworthy."

As Julia hurried away, she was unaware that young Stephen was holding his cheek in a reverent manner. The coins were a precious gift, but Stephen was convinced that the kiss was of even greater worth.

Chapter Three

Taryn stood on a rocky outcropping and surveyed the lush, green countryside spread out before him. As far as the eye could see, there were gently rolling hills with a few small copses of trees sprinkled here and there. The leaves on the trees currently reflected the reddish glow of the setting sun.

To the south, the view wasn't of hills and trees but of a large wetland that, in this area, marked the separation between Scotland and the northern border of Britain. Although this wasn't a classically beautiful view, Taryn still found the gnarled trees and marshy land equally interesting to behold. They contained their own beauty and emitted a sense of the mystery that was Scotland. Even now, Taryn felt a presence that was familiar to him; he knew it as the free and wild spirit of the land. Its majesty and power drew him in and made him realize, once again, how strong his love for the country was. Even though he was miles south of his home in Edinburgh, it didn't matter. All of Scotland was his home and he would fight to protect it.

His final turn in his survey was to the scene in the west. Here, the stunning view was marred by the debris from the battle which had recently been fought. Parts of armor and damaged swords lay scattered on the field. In one area, he spotted a portion of a standard which had been torn and left behind by one of his men.

Taryn thought back on the skirmish that had occurred earlier today. He replayed the entire battle in his mind, making note of the things he could have done differently and deciding what he would discuss with his officers when they met later this evening. Overall, he was pleased. His men had fought well and casualties had been few. His father would be pleased as well when he made his report.

He was brought out of his reverie by the familiar cry of the Hawk. He looked up to see Skye circling above as she looked for a place to land nearby. Spying an ideal place, he indicated the large boulder to her even as he moved closer to it himself. She landed gracefully and carefully placed a small pouch beside her on the rock.

A present for you. She indicated the pouch with her beak.

Taryn was afraid to hope. *Is it what I think it is?*

The poison that was used on the sword.

Taryn was flabbergasted. *Skye, how did you ever manage to get this?*

Skye preened. **A girl needs to keep some secrets, Taryn.**

You are truly amazing.

Thank you. Should I take it to Julia?

Taryn shot Skye a disgusted look. *I don't need Julia for this. I can figure out what was placed in here and devise an antidote based on the ingredients.*

Perhaps you should let Julia do this. It's more her forte than yours.

Skye, I am perfectly capable of doing this.

I know that Taryn, but she is even more capable. I just don't want to see your pride cause you to take a foolish chance with your life.

Taryn sighed. *All right, I admit that some of this is about pride, but I also want to keep Julia from worrying.*

And interfering.

Exactly!

All right. But if this doesn't work, I'll tell Julia myself.

Taryn was smug as he questioned her. *How? You can't talk to her unless I facilitate the link.*

No. But I can take a flight which will put me in range of Reggie. Skye paused briefly for effect. **We both know that when Reggie knows...**

Taryn joined in and completed the thought with Skye, *...Julia knows!* He groaned and half-jokingly thought, *Traitor!*

Skye quickly grabbed the pouch, which was beside her, and backed out of his reach. She directed her angry thoughts at him. **What did you say?**

He tried to placate her. *C'mon Skye. I was only joking. I know that you would never betray me.*

She glared at him through the eyes of a predator and held her position.

Taryn, who was a bit baffled by her extreme reaction, quickly tried to undo his misstep. *All right. I'm sorry. I should never have said that.*

Skye waited.

What more do you want? He stared at her. Then, realizing the answer to his own question, he took a deep breath and began the often-recited refrain. *Skye, you know I couldn't do any of this without you. I am deeply sorry if I offended you, and I beg your forgiveness.*

After a final beady-eyed glare, Skye finally relented, walked regally to his side, and deposited the bag by his hand. **That's better.**

Taryn snatched the bag up before he projected his thoughts. *Women! You're all alike.*

Skye let out a shriek that sounded like a cackle. **You only say that because you can't win against us.** With that, she launched herself into the air. **Enough of this nonsense. I'm heading back to the British camp. Something is brewing over there, and I'm going to find out exactly what is going on.**

Taryn smiled. *Okay, you win this round. And despite your abuse, I'm truly grateful.*

I know you are, Taryn. Be sure to give Julia and Reggie my best.

As he watched his ally fly south toward the British camp, Taryn wondered what it was that Skye had picked up on that was happening over there. He knew that she would come to him as soon as she had anything specific to report, but her instincts coupled with his own forced him to acknowledge that the British were indeed stepping up their attack. First the poison, and now something else.

If only his father would finally give him leave to stage an attack, rather than constantly ordering him to attempt parley which was futile. He was only allowed to fight to defend against encroachment by the enemy. Perhaps the report of today's attack with the poison would sway him.

Taryn was leading the army on behalf of his father, Lord Johann, who ruled over the lands in southern Scotland from his castle in Edinburgh. Johann was a kind and beloved monarch whose reign was being challenged by Lord Royce, an English Lord who was looking to expand his territory north into Scottish country.

Johann and Taryn had vowed to do everything they could to stop Royce from taking over the land they both loved so dearly. Despite his fatherly misgivings and fears, Johann had sent his untested child and only son to lead the army and stop Royce's advance. That decision was turning out to be a fortuitous one. Even though he was only twenty-one years old and hardly a seasoned warrior, Taryn was proving himself to be a valiant young man with good leadership qualities.

As a boy, he had been trained in the art of fighting in addition to his schooling as an enchanter and a healer. Even though this was his first opportunity to use his fighting skills in the field, Taryn had discovered that he had been served well by his training and that he had a good head on his shoulders for strategy. Of course, it didn't hurt that his father had sent Scotland's best war strategists and advisors to the battlefront with him. Yet, even with crediting the fine skills of the advisors, Taryn still knew that he was the one whom the men followed. It was as if they sensed in him a kinship in his determination to protect the land and his family. This, coupled with his natural ability to lead and his own willingness to fight and risk himself, made for an inspiring leader and a united army.

As he headed back to camp, his thoughts were all focused on how he might convince his father to let him take the offensive and attack Royce's men. Taryn was certain that he could triumph if his father would allow him to lead as he saw fit. He was anxious to end this war and return to the life he had left behind in Edinburgh. He had people back home who were waiting for his return and whom he was longing to see.

Chapter Four

The wind whistled through her drafty room in the west turret of the castle, yet Julia barely noticed as she paced by the fire and silently cursed her brother. Damn him. Where the hell was he? He knew that she waited at this time each night to hear from him. Maybe she had been wrong earlier today, and his injury had been worse than she thought. Julia had opened the firelink over an hour ago and had been wearing a path pacing the castle floor ever since.

Like her brother, Julia was tall, slender, and attractive. Her coloring differed from Taryn's, as she favored their mother's side of the family while he favored the lighter coloring of their father's. Her long auburn hair usually hung loose to her waist, although she often tied the sides back when working so that it wouldn't annoy her or interfere with her field of vision. Her hazel eyes were equally as intelligent and focused as her brother's blue ones, although her gaze was often far more serious in nature.

It wasn't only their coloring and age difference that separated Julia and her younger brother. Where Taryn was adventurous and sometimes reckless, Julia was planned and steady. While Julia was fierce in her belief about proper preparation before their enchantment work, Taryn was relaxed and trusting of his skills. Although these differences were sometimes the source of frustration and small arguments between them, they were generally tolerant of each other and had grown to view their personal quirks as sources of amusement and teasing over the years. They knew that they were like flip sides of the same coin and, over the years, they had learned to respect each other's abilities and to work well as a team. Except when one half of the team was aggravated with the other, such as right now.

At this moment, Julia was focused solely on her brother's annoying traits. Foremost among these was the fact that sometimes Taryn could be so caught up in his own world that he was oblivious to everyone else around him. At these times, he was completely self-centered, forgetting that others were counting on him. Forgetting that **she** was counting on him. This penchant had been true even more of late as he had recently been spending a great deal of time with his latest lover, Shira.

Julia smiled in smug satisfaction as she realized that there was no chance of that tonight; she knew that he was safe from that woman right now. Ironically, that was the one positive aspect of Taryn's being away from Edinburgh. He was away from Shira. That meant that the only possible dangers in his life at the moment were a raging battle that could still be taking place with Royce's men, and the one that was going to erupt if he ignored his sister much longer.

Julia sighed and tried to calm her churning emotions. Deep down, she knew that her anger and frustration were really masking her fear and worry; she didn't know what she would do if anything ever happened to her brother. She had spent hours worrying about him fighting on the battlefield and doing everything in her power to protect him. The only thing she asked of him was that he check in with her each night and let her see for herself that he was safe. That really wasn't asking too much.

"Julia? Are you there?"

She turned and looked into the fire where she saw her brother's image appear before her. "High time, Taryn. Where have you been?"

Her brother's face wavered and steadied as the flames in the fireplace flickered in the evening light. "For Heaven's sake, it's not as if I'm just sitting around doing nothing. I **am** in the middle of a battlefield out here."

Julia sighed as she acknowledged his words. "I know Tay, but **you** know how worried I get if I have to wait to hear from you. I imagine all sorts of possible things that could've gone wrong. Speaking of which, what happened to your shoulder?"

Taryn groaned inwardly. He knew that he'd never keep it from her. "Nothing much. Just a small scrape. Gern and I cleaned it earlier."

Julia squinted at him to assure herself that he was telling the truth. When she didn't see anything to indicate otherwise, she relented. "All right. It looked fine when I checked in on you this afternoon."

"Thanks. I felt you working in my energy field. It's not as sore any more."

"You know if you need me, you can let me know. It always takes you so long to tell me what's going on down there."

"Calm down, Julia. It's just a scrape. You worry too much."

She sighed in acknowledgement. "Well, it's not as if that's going to change. What kept you so long tonight?"

"I had to do a final check on the perimeter of the camp and then wait for the rest of the men to leave my campfire area and retire to their own tents. I don't think many would understand our form of communication. They already think it odd that I can predict the enemy's strategies on such a consistent basis." Taryn paused. "And speaking of that, what news have you from the British camp? Did you send Reggie as I requested?"

"I did and she reports that Lord Royce's men are readying a surprise attack. They plan to outmaneuver you from the south side."

"Impossible!" Taryn's reaction was immediate. "There's a large swamp to our south." He shook his head in denial. "The Rook must be misinformed."

Julia bristled at her brother's remark and rose to her ally's defense. "Hah! When have you known her to be wrong? If you were going to doubt her, you should have sent the Hawk."

Taryn, realizing that he had stepped on his sister's sensitive toes, tried to placate her. "I told you. Skye is working on something else for me. She's gathering some important information. Information which could be big enough to swing the tide of this war in our favor."

"And something that you evidently can't share with your sister." Julia's hurt was apparent in the tone of her response.

"I actually don't have much to share yet. I've just felt the energy building in the British camp. Skye has gone to get the specific information I need in order to act. When I learn more, you'll be the first to know."

"Or the second…or the third…"

She was ticking the numbers off on her fingers and Taryn quickly changed the subject before she could build up a full head of steam. "What else from the Rook?"

Julia switched subjects as seamlessly as he had. "Evidently Royce's men have been secretly scouting out a safe path through the swamp and have finally come upon one. The fact that you have had such dry weather has placed them at an advantage as the swamp is less, well, swampy."

Taryn thought for a moment and then shrugged off the threat. "Let them come if they want. We'll deal with them when they get here. **If** they get here."

Julia looked at her brother in frustration. "A little advance planning wouldn't kill you, Tay."

As usual when his sister irritated him, Taryn ignored her. "What news of home? Is Phaelon still giving you grief?"

"Ach. He's just an old wizard. Nothing I can't handle. It will take more than some simple tricks to fool me."

Taryn's brow creased. "Don't underestimate him, Julia. He still has some power left in those weary bones. And he still has some friends in the court."

"I know. But I have friends, too. And so do you." She smiled at her brother to allay his concerns. "We'll be fine."

The fire flickered as the communication came to end. She hated saying goodbye to him, but knew that he needed time to rest and plan the next day's war strategy. There was one more question that she was sure he would ask before severing the firelink. "Um… I was wondering if you've seen Shira?"

She knew it was difficult for him to ask this last question as Shira was often the sticking point between them. Lately, they had spent more hours arguing about that woman than anything else. "She's fine." Taryn waited for more, but Julia would give him nothing. "That's all I'll say."

He sighed, frustrated by his sister's attitude when it came to Shira. "Okay. Give her my regards."

Snapping at him, she said, "Give them yourself when you return. And try to make it soon." She softened her tone. "I miss you when you aren't here. You're the only human I can count on to always have my back."

He knew that was true for him, as well. "Okay. Wish me luck and send some energy for tomorrow. See you in the evening."

She smiled at him. "You know I always wish you luck." She looked at him closely and saw the strain of the past few days on his face. "Get some sleep. See you after sunset." Julia suddenly realized she should remind her brother of the plans they had discussed a few days earlier. "Oh, and Tay, don't forget we'll be on our way to Sarah's. We leave tomorrow morning."

"I didn't forget. It's not a moment too soon."

"Why? Have you gotten any more information?"

"No. Nothing more than the initial dream. It just repeats in various ways. Thomas is always either trapped somewhere or being slowly pulled out of my reach."

Julia's lips set in a firm line. "That will never happen."

Taryn smiled at her. "If I can't protect him myself, there's no one else I'd rather have watching him."

"Thanks Tay. You know how much I love him."

"I do. And I also I know that I don't need to tell **you** to be careful."

Julia smiled in return. "No, I think I've got everything pretty much covered."

"And then some, I'm sure. See you tomorrow night."

For just a moment as the siblings were saying their final good-byes, Julia thought she saw another face appear briefly in the flames. Oddly enough, it had happened once or twice before as well, and it always seemed to be the same man.

She paused, wondering if she should mention it to Taryn the next time they spoke. Maybe she should reestablish the link and call him back. She shook her head as she realized he would only tease her about it and tell her to stop worrying.

Fine. She would take his advice and do just that. Most likely it was one of Taryn's men who had passed by just as they were releasing the link. Reassured, she turned back to the more pressing tasks at hand. It probably wasn't all that important anyway.

Chapter Five

After having one more brief conversation, Taryn turned from the fire and went off to locate Gern. He would have Gern place a few soldiers by the entrance to the swamp at once. Royce's men weren't going to take him by surprise. He shook his head as he realized that once again, Julia had been on top of the latest developments at the battle site. God, that was annoying.

He supposed that this time it was his fault. For once, he had asked her to send the Rook to the enemy camp while the Hawk was otherwise involved. But there were several other times in the past when she had sent Reggie uninvited to check on him. Why couldn't she just back off and trust him to lead the army? It wasn't as if they had been losing ground under his command. Actually, they had been defending themselves well in the minor skirmishes that had occurred thus far and had been ably preventing any advance on Royce's part.

As Taryn greeted the different groups of men that he passed, he reflected on his relationship with his sister. He knew that, above all, he and Julia loved each other. They were connected in ways which neither could fully explain or understand. Indeed, they would die to protect each other and Taryn's son, Thomas.

He also knew that much of the recent tension between them stemmed from their concern for each other. It was rare for them to be apart and working on separate paths when they were faced with so much danger. Even though they had frequently studied apart as children, they always worked together when times were troubled. Early on in their training, it had become apparent to both of them that their combined powers were far greater than the sum of their parts. That meant that any direct threat, severe illness, or other challenge requiring their skills as healers and enchanters was best tackled with a united front. Which made this current situation not only unusual but uncomfortable.

In fairness, he realized that it must be difficult for Julia to be the one who was left behind at home; he was the one taking all of the risks on the battlefield. He would have hated that if the roles had been reversed.

Yet, acknowledging her warranted frustrations, as well as his love for her, still didn't prevent Taryn from also acknowledging how aggravating she could be. Why couldn't she just ease up and trust? He knew that they were both capable of handling whatever came their way.

Taryn entered the tent where Gern was involved in an intense card game with some of his fellow officers.

Gern looked up at his approach. "How's the shoulder?"

"Better."

"Ready to join in for the next hand? I could stand to have someone around who I always beat."

"Hah! Did you catch the latest fever Gern? I can't recall ever losing to you."

Gern laughed. "Well there's always a first time. Pull up a log."

Taryn looked fondly at the large man and asked, "Have you assigned the guard for tonight?"

"Just took care of it."

"We need to assign two more to the swamp entrance."

Gern shot his boss a puzzled look. "The swamp entrance? Why would we need to cover that?"

Taryn gave Gern a clear, steady look and said, "A little bird told me that there may be some action that way."

Gern, immediately understanding Taryn's unspoken message, placed his cards on the table, stood, and replied, "I'll see to it at once."

"Okay. While you're gone, I'll keep your seat warm," Taryn joked as he claimed the log on which Gern had recently been perched and picked up Gern's cards.

"Great. There goes that hand." Gern rolled his eyes and shook his head as he left the tent with the men's laughter echoing behind him.

Chapter Six

As Julia turned away from the fire, she reflected on her sharp response to Taryn's question about Shira. She hated it when they bickered, but there was something about Shira that really stuck in her craw. Every time she even thought about the woman, Julia swore that she could hear warning bells sounding in the distance.

Julia knew with every fiber of her being that the woman was going to be her brother's undoing, and she'd be damned if she stood by and watched it happen. The only reason it had gone on this long was that Julia hesitated to use her magic against Shira. It just didn't seem right, not to mention that Taryn would kill her if he ever found out.

Julia sighed and moved her hair back from her face. If Shira kept pushing her luck, then Julia would just have to do something about her. She hoped it wouldn't come to that, but she'd never stand by idly and watch while anyone hurt her brother.

Shira and Taryn had met while Taryn was grieving the death of his wife, Celia, who had succumbed to a fever that swept through Edinburgh a few years earlier. Celia had been a beautiful, gentle, loving wife to Taryn and a dear friend to Julia, as well. The couple had one son, Thomas, who was currently five and safe in the castle with Julia and his nanny Margret, the same nanny who had helped to raise Julia and Taryn. The fact that Taryn hadn't asked for Thomas didn't worry Julia, as she knew the devoted father always checked in on his son by other means. No bedtime was complete without a little gift or note from Dad. Thomas always waited anxiously to hear from his father before going to bed.

"Julia, Julia. Look what Father sent me!" Thomas appeared at her door holding a carved bow and a quiver full of arrows. His small face was an exact duplicate of his father's at that age and currently reflected a look of pure joy and excitement. He raced into the room and hurtled his small body onto Julia's bed almost piercing the thick feather mattress with one of the arrows.

"Good Grief, TomCat. Watch where you're pointing that thing!" Thomas wasn't fooled for an instant by Julia's mock gruff tone. He knew that she was a devoted aunt who thought that the sun rose and set on him. He could've been spoiled with all of the attention that he had lavished on him, but he wasn't. Not only was he a loving, generous little boy, but he was clearly showing some of the family talent in the art of enchantment. With Taryn's approval, Julia had been secretly coaching him and developing his fledgling skills. It had to be kept a secret because neither she nor Taryn wanted Phaelon teaching Thomas.

At one time, Taryn and Julia had both trained at the feet of the Court Minister, Phaelon. Phaelon was a moderately skilled healer and magician who had become more and more bitter and devious as time went on. What started as an amicable relationship between a teacher and his students had soured as Phaelon saw his own ambitions to be Lord Johann's right hand man usurped by his growing charges.

As the father listened to his children more and more, he listened to Phaelon less and less and the old man had become resentful and nasty. His outward appearance had also changed over the years to reflect his sour disposition. He was tall and wiry by nature, but his more recent habits of skulking about the halls of the castle and wearing an old black robe which was torn and dirty lent him a sinister air. Both Julia and Taryn had a healthy sense of distrust when it came to Phaelon.

The only reason that Phaelon was still at court was because their father felt he owed him loyalty for all of the years of service. Julia thought that was a weakness on her father's part, but she kept her mouth shut. Besides, Phaelon was rarely more than a nuisance; he didn't seem a real threat to her no matter what Taryn said. Even with that, he wasn't getting anywhere near her nephew.

Julia had always been quick to defend and protect those whom she loved. Perhaps this was due to their mother's death when she and Taryn were still quite young. In her childish way, Julia had done her best to fill the role of protector and nurturer for her brother even though their age difference was so slight. By now, she was so used to the role that she didn't even realize that she was still playing it. What she did realize was that she never wanted to lose another person that she loved; thus, she always did her best to assure herself of their safety. And Julia knew that the most effective way of doing this was through her work as an enchanter.

~~~~~~~~~~~~~~~

Julia had shown an early talent for magic and, by the age of five, was concocting all sorts of simple spells on her own. This was unbeknownst to any save for her brother who was quick to follow in his older sister's footsteps. Their father discovered his progeny's skills by accident one day when he came upon seven-year-old Taryn peering into the downstairs hearth as he spoke to his sister whose face appeared in the flames. Johann stood in shock for a few minutes trying to digest this altered reality while the siblings chatted, oblivious of his presence. As he approached the hearth and his young son, his daughter spotted him and greeted him calmly.

"Oh, hello Father."

"H-h-h-hello," Johann stuttered. "Where are you?" he asked as he leaned to peer into the hearth.

Julia giggled at her father's obvious confusion. "I'm in my room Daddy. Taryn just wanted to ask me a question."

Johann, struggling to regain his equanimity, said, "Oh. Of course. Well, carry on."

With that, he stood off to one side and waited as the siblings bid each other farewell. When the conversation was finished and Julia's countenance had disappeared from the fire, he questioned his young son.

"Taryn, do you and Julia always talk that way?"

Taryn thought the answer was obvious, but he humored his father. "Only when we're not together, Dad."

"But how did you learn to do that?"

Taryn frowned as he tried to recall the beginning of something that he had been doing for much of his young life. "One day, when I was working on a potion, I got really mad when it wouldn't come out right. I looked all over for Julia to help me, but I couldn't find her anywhere."

Johann prompted his son with a quizzical look. "And then what happened?"

"I was so mad I threw the herbs into the fire and yelled Julia's name over and over, until suddenly, she was there." He pointed his finger toward the flames.

Johann, fearing for his son's safety, said, "Ah Taryn, you do realize she's not in the fire, don't you?"

Taryn looked at his father as if he had lost all sense. "Well, of course, Dad. She told you - she's in her room."

"Of course." Johann quickly realized that he was in over his head and went off in search of wiser council. His first instinct was to discuss the matter with the children's nanny who spent a great amount of time in their company. When he questioned Nanny Margret later in the day, she professed ignorance of the hearth chats but did verify another startling ability.

"No sir, I've never seen the fire chats. Thank Heavens no one was burned!"

"Indeed. Have you seen anything else unusual, Nanny?"

Nanny Magret looked a bit uncomfortable. "Well, sir, I never thought to mention it before. I just thought they'd outgrow it. Most children do."

Johann's impatience was growing, but he worked to remain calm. "Well?"

"They play this game where they hurtle objects at each other."

"What kind of objects?"

"Fruit. Twigs. Anything within reach that's not too heavy." Johann frowned and Nanny misread the reason for it. "Don't worry, sir. These games always end in laughter. It's just another of their competitions. You know how they are. They would never hurt each other."

"Nanny, I know that."

"Besides, most children outgrow these abilities. They just fade as they age."

"Nanny, I'm afraid you've got me confused. How is the ability to toss an apple across a room anything special?"

Nanny's eyes widened as she suddenly understood Johann's confusion.

"They don't use their hands to throw, sir."

"What?"

"It's true." Nanny then demonstrated as she spoke. "They just wave their little hands at an object across the room and the next thing you know, it has smacked into the head of the other."

Johann frowned. "I see. That **is** different."

"I should say so."

As Johann tried to absorb this additional information, he supposed that he should be grateful for their strong bond. At least he didn't have to worry about their hurtling dangerous objects at one another.

Still, this new discovery left him in a predicament. Clearly, the children had a gift which could be developed. Indeed, if their gift was for healing as well as magic, (which was sometimes the case) they could be helpful to the people of the land. The children's mother, Johann's wife Louisa, had died in childbirth because there was no resident healer available at the time. It was this memory more than anything else which helped Johann decide that he should support the children's gifts with the proper training. After a few months of searching, he finally found Phaelon and brought him to Edinburgh.

~~~~~~~~~~~~~~~

Phaelon arrived with strong credentials. He had trained for years under the Druids in northern Scotland and was considered well versed in both enchantment and healing work. What Johann didn't know was that while well trained, Phaelon was only moderately talented. This would become painfully evident as his young charges eclipsed him during the first few years. The other thing that Johann didn't know was that Phaelon had a carefully hidden desire for power.

Because of this desire, Phaelon was quick to accept the job under Johann, the Lord with the largest land mass in Scotland. Indeed Johann's castle in Edinburgh was located in a very advantageous position on the top of a hillside overlooking miles of open land. A surprise attack on the castle was downright difficult, if not impossible. A superior location, coupled with peasant fealty for years of good treatment and care, had kept Johann as the strongest and most beloved Lord in Scotland. To Phaelon's way of thinking, this also made him an ideal employer.

In many outward respects, Phaelon had been dealt the winning hand in this partnership. His work obligations were few, and as his students surpassed him, there was less and less required of him. Soon, Julia and Taryn were seeking out other more skilled teachers, and Phaelon was left to his own devices and given plenty of free time.

Although this would appear an easy and ideal life, inwardly Phaelon's resentment grew. Over time, feeling disrespected and unneeded had soured his disposition and made him bitter. He had started to retaliate in the only way he knew how. At first, he tried to cause trouble in the family relationships. He would tell lies to Johann about his children or try to pit Taryn and Julia against each other; however, they quickly became wise to this and no longer rose to the bait.

So Phaelon started to cause trouble in other ways. Potions were spoiled, doors were left unbolted, belongings were rifled through and magical items went missing. Initially, this had proven to be a hindrance to the siblings, but they quickly learned to place protective spells around items and to be more secretive about hiding their belongings. In the end, Phaelon was only a minor irritation, and while they would have preferred him gone, they didn't expend much energy worrying about him.

Chapter Seven

Back in her room, Julia stopped her musings on Phaelon and joined Thomas who had ventured onto the balcony to play with his new gift. When he had successfully, if not skillfully, launched an arrow, she applauded and cheered.

"Well done, Thomas." The young boy beamed up at her. "Some day you'll be as good as your dad at archery, but it'll take at least a few more hours of practice." She winked at her nephew. "I think that's enough for now. The hour's late and it's time for you to settle down and get ready for bed." Julia ushered her nephew back inside and went to sit on the bed.

"Aw, Julia, do I have to?" Even as he said it, he knew what the answer was and climbed up to sit beside her.

"Yes, but I have a surprise planned for tomorrow that you can think about as you drift off to sleep tonight." She gently lifted his chin so he was looking into her eyes. "We're going on an adventure."

"Really?" His blue eyes shone brightly as he tried to decide what might be in store for him. Aunt Julia was usually quite good with surprises, so he thought that it must be something fun. "Can we ride Firefly?"

"Yes. We will need the horse to get there."

"Is it far?"

"Farther than you've ever been."

"Will Father be there?"

"Not this time, but your dad has been there on many occasions, and he said that I could take you there tomorrow."

Thomas' eyes lit up, and he bounced on the bed as he begged, "Please, Julia, tell me where."

"We're going to see a very wise friend of mine who will teach you lots of secrets about working with plants and roots. She'll show you how to make medicine to help heal people."

He looked at her in surprise. "But I want you to teach me, Julia."

"I will still teach you, Thomas, but Sarah is a very skilled healer and herbalist. You're lucky that she's agreed to work with you. It's very rare for her to take on a new student these days."

Julia continued, "As you know, Thomas, you will have to help with the healing for the people of the land when you grow up. Until then, you'll have all different kinds of training and will even be able to work with the Druids to learn a variety of skills. Sarah is only the first of many teachers who will assist you on your path." She paused and looked at her nephew who was still so young. "Some day you'll be responsible for the jobs that your father and I do, because we'll be too old to do them."

Thomas studied her face. "When will that be?"

She laughed and mussed his hair, as she said, "Not for a while I hope. We still have a few good years left in us."

He looked at her seriously, and said, "Okay, Julia. Because I'm still only five, you know."

"I know, Thomas." She smiled fondly at the young child who was so dear to her heart. "Now off to bed with you. Five-year-olds need lots of sleep. Ask Nanny Margret to tell you a story."

"Can Tiger be in my story? He hates it when she leaves him out."

"Absolutely. Ask Nanny to put Tiger in your story."

"Okay. Night, Julia." He leaned over to kiss her on the cheek.

"Night, TomCat."

~~~~~~~~~~~~~~~

As she watched her nephew race from the room, Julia mused over the initial discovery of the boy's potential. It had been far less dramatic than her father's discovery of her and Taryn speaking through the flames in the hearth, and was the reason for Julia's affectionate nickname for the boy of TomCat.

Once he started to talk, Thomas would often be found chatting in empty rooms. At first Nanny thought he might be talking to himself, and later she assumed he had an imaginary friend. All in all, she thought the habit endearing and nothing to fuss over. When she casually mentioned this habit to Taryn and Julia, they immediately suspected the truth. Thomas had been

34

chatting with his power animal, Tiger, all along. The little boy saw him almost as clearly as they could see each other.

Since that discovery, Thomas had evidenced a growing interest in the healing arts. He loved being outdoors and always asked about the natural world. Even at five, he could readily identify the local trees and plants. If Thomas' future were to be as an enchanter or healer, then it was not too early to begin his training. Taryn and Julia had taught him some of the basics, but he was ready to learn more. This, coupled with Taryn's vague yet worrisome dream, was the reason for tomorrow's journey.

Before retiring for the evening, Julia would do all that she could to assure their safe passage through the forest that led to Sarah's home. She went back out onto the balcony to summon the Rook to review the plans for tomorrow's journey. Because Nanny was older and unable to travel for too long without significant discomfort, it would take two days to reach Sarah's house. Julia had debated whether she and Thomas would be safer sleeping in the woods or at an inn. She decided to check in with her allies for advice.

Over the years, Julia and Taryn had both learned a variety of ways to communicate with each other and their animal allies. In order to converse so that none could overhear, they honed a skill which they referred to as a mindlink. To do this, they had to quiet their minds, focus their thoughts, and send out a clear intention to link or communicate with the chosen one. That clear intention presented itself via language or pictures in the mind of the other person or animal ally. Then he or she responded by also intending to communicate, and the link was created.

After that, they simply held a conversation in their heads as opposed to out loud. They found that they could hear each other quite clearly, and others could not hear them at all unless they were intentionally included in the link. The only downside was that the efficacy of the link was directly impacted by distance. If the parties were too far apart, it was difficult, if not impossible, to establish.

That, however, was not the case right now as Julia quieted her mind and focused on a certain bird that usually resided in the forest at the edge of the grounds. Julia could sense her flying over the castle and before much time elapsed, their minds connected and the Rook, whom Julia had named Reggie, or more formally Regina, landed lightly beside her on the parapet.

Hello, friend. I wanted to review our plans for the journey tomorrow.

Julia, you are extremely worried about this trip. Do you sense some danger?

Nothing specific, but Taryn's dream does have me worried.

It is disconcerting.

And there is danger all around us these days. One can't be too careful.

I understand. Royce is determined to win your father's land at all costs. What can I do to help?

You can scout ahead and assure me that the path is clear. If we need to suddenly change direction or hide, let me know as soon as possible. Nothing can happen to Thomas. He is our future. He must be kept safe.

Of course, Julia. No harm will come to any of you.

Good. I trust you, Reggie. I'm just nervous about taking Thomas off the grounds. I'll also ask the Wolf and her pack to journey with us and let us know if they scent anything on the ground. In that way, we'll cover both land and air.

Yes, Reggie tilted her head and looked at Julia, **but warn them to keep out of sight. The last time one was spotted, he almost lost his life to the coachman's arrow.**

Julia nodded as she recalled the incident in question. *I think the wolf cub learned his lesson from that experience, but I'll remind them.*

Have you decided where you'll spend the night?

I'm debating the merits of each of my possible choices. Obviously Nanny will need to stay at an inn. I'm thinking that it's best if Thomas and I sleep in the woods. That way no innkeeper or guests will remember us or know in which direction we were headed. It seems that this is a time for us to use all the precautions available. The fewer people who can trace our whereabouts, the better.

36

What about the coachmen? Surely they will know where you are.

I've already made plans for that, my friend.

Reggie fluffed her wings out and squawked in what could only be interpreted as a rook's version of a laugh. **I'm sure you have.**

Julia grimaced at her ally. *Oh Reggie. Don't you give me a hard time, too.*

Very well. Reggie turned to look out over the castle grounds. **You know that the Wolf and I would also prefer the woods as we can keep you safer when you're on our turf.**

Julia, who had already been leaning toward the same decision, agreed. *That settles it then. Thomas and I will sleep in the clearing near the fairy bower in Settler's Woods.*

Good. I'll be back at first light. I'm going a bit farther into the forest to hunt tonight. Reggie fluffed her wings and looked at Julia. **Care to join me for a short flight?**

I'd love to, but I want to contact the Wolf and make sure that she knows about our plans for the morrow. Until then, be well.

You too, Julia.

Julia watched Reggie take flight and head to the forest before she summoned the Wolf who agreed on the plan for the journey to Sarah's. The wolf pack would not only accompany them on the trip but would remain in the forest around Sarah's house while Julia, Thomas and Nanny were in residence. With everything that she could possibly control completed, Julia finally retired to bed and fell into a deep, restful sleep.

Chapter Eight

Miles away, Taryn also slept deeply, and as he did, he dreamed of his son, Thomas. They were back at the castle playing a spirited game of hide and seek and it was Thomas's turn to hide. Taryn counted slowly to twenty and then opened his eyes, "Here I come!"

He heard childish giggling coming from behind the very large and suddenly lumpy tapestry that was hanging in the main hall. Taryn decided to let his son have some fun, so he wandered around the area. "Thomas, where are you? Thomas?" He muttered softly, as he searched, "Now where is that young man? He really has hidden himself away from me this time." More giggles came from the wall hanging.

"Hmmm, maybe he's here." He moved a chair a few feet over. "No, not there." He wandered a bit closer to his son. "Maybe here." He searched inside a standing suit of armor. "No, not there either." He moved closer to his son. "I know where he is, he's here!" With that, he pulled back the tapestry in triumph.

Suddenly there was a blinding flash of lightning and Taryn found himself outdoors in a violent storm. Chaos had erupted all around him. The noise was fierce as thunder crashed and the wind whipped leaves, branches and small stones at him.

"Father! Father!" He somehow heard Thomas' frightened voice above the noise.

"Thomas, where are you?"

Lightening hit nearby and illuminated Thomas. He was holding onto the tender branches of a sapling as the storm roared around him.

"Hold tight, Son. I'm coming." Taryn struggled to reach his son while wind-blown projectiles tried to stop him. His progress was painstakingly slow, but finally he neared Thomas who reached out to grasp Taryn's outstretched hand. Lightning flashed between them and Taryn was blinded for an instant. When he could finally see again, Thomas was gone. "Thomas! Thomas!" He shrieked over and over above the howling winds.

Taryn awoke drenched in sweat and filled with fear. His heart was pounding as he sat up. He rubbed his hands over his face trying to remove himself from the tense world of the dream and come back to reality. "Thomas is safe. He's with Julia. You just spoke to him. You know he's safe." He repeated various versions of this mantra over and over until he could feel his head clear and his pulse return to normal.

When Taryn was somewhat calmer, he turned his attention back to the dream. It was yet another version of the recently recurring theme. Thomas was always lost or taken from him. No matter how much he mulled it over, Taryn couldn't uncover anything beyond the obvious in this new version of the dream.

Taryn had been working with his dreams for years, and he had always gotten excellent insights and information from them. Past experience had taught him that when a dream recurred, there was some pivotal piece of information he had yet to glean. But no matter how hard he tried, Taryn just couldn't figure out what this dream was trying to tell him that he didn't already know. Thomas was in danger. But weren't they all in this time of war? And Taryn knew that he was doing all he possibly could to keep his son safe. If he could just uncover more of the clues in the dream, perhaps he could do even more.

Although it seemed counter-intuitive, Taryn knew that sometimes the best way to uncover something was to stop thinking about it for a while. He decided to clear his head with a run and then try again. Maybe then he would figure out why he kept having the same dream over and over again and what more he needed to do to keep his son safe.

Chapter Nine

The Stag and his companion strolled through the forest munching on leaves and enjoying the early morning sunshine playing though the branches of the trees. They had just completed a forest run, and he felt good. He enjoyed pushing and testing his physical limits and remembering what his body could do. Furthermore, he loved the sense of freedom that came with this type of pursuit. For a short time, his mind was focused on only one thing: his successful run. All other worries were momentarily swept away.

His companion stamped her hoof loudly and caught his attention. He looked over just as she glanced upward. The Stag recognized the signal and looked up to see Skye circling above him. The Hawk landed on a tree branch and greeted him.

Good Morning. I hope you had a nice run, because it's time for business. We need to fly over the British camp. There is some activity that I want you to see for yourself.

The Stag sighed; free time was a thing of the past for him these days. And how he missed it too. Ah well. He supposed that he should be happy that he had enjoyed some time with his four-legged companion. Although he hadn't unlocked any more of the dream's code, the run had helped him to put it into perspective. Once again, he trusted that its meaning would become clear in time for him to act. Until then, he would do all that he could to keep Thomas safe.

He said goodbye to his fellow deer, thanking her for the early morning camaraderie, and prepared for the shapeshift. At this point in his practice, he didn't have to become human again before becoming a Hawk. He could morph smoothly from one animal to the next as long as he kept his focus.

Slowly, he entered the Hawk's mind and began to feel his thoughts align with those of a bird of prey. He felt his face take shape first. The eyes became smaller and sharper, the nose became a beak. Then he felt his hooves separate into talons and his forelegs become wings. After a short time, the transition was complete, and Taryn flew up to join Skye on the tree branch. The deer bade them a good flight as she wandered off to find some sweeter leaves to munch.

What news, Skye?

The British are buzzing about something. It appears that their captain, Carlson, has been gifted with a magical sword. It has been enchanted by a powerful wizard, and Carlson is said to be undefeatable while he holds that sword.

Taryn's eyes sparkled. *Really. Now **that** is an interesting development.* He could feel his excitement grow as it always did when he was faced with a new challenge. *Finally something I can sink my claws into. What are we waiting for? Let's go.*

Wait. There's more. Skye called out to her human charge, but it was too late. He was already off and heading toward the enemy camp. She would have to warn him of the dangers that lay ahead. If only he weren't so impulsive sometimes. Ah well. It kept her on her talons, that's for sure. Now she would have to really employ some speed to catch him.

~~~~~~~~~~~~~~~~

From a nearby nest he had temporarily commandeered, the Sparrow watched Skye try to catch up with her partner. Even though he wasn't privy to the mindlink between the two, he was pretty confident that he knew what had just transpired. It also appeared that, once again, Taryn had acted rashly and flown off without all of the information. The Sparrow knew that it really didn't matter if Skye caught up to Taryn and warned him of what she knew. There was plenty of information that she would never uncover - not until it was too late.

The tiny bird decided to take a little sightseeing journey of his own and flew out of the nest perched high up in the tree. Rather than heading towards the British camp, a place he had been to on many occasions, he set a course north toward the castle in Edinburgh. As he enjoyed his leisurely flight, he wondered what he would find when he arrived. It was time to uncover what Julia was up to and to visit a certain young lady who lived nearby.

He realized, as he had often in the past, that he was truly delighting in this little game that he had devised and was looking forward to the moment when the players found out that they had been his pawns all along. He would enjoy bringing the children of his enemy to their knees. They were worthy adversaries, but he knew how to best them all the same.

The Sparrow had lived the past several years of his life planning strategies to reach that final moment when Johann and his family line were irrevocably destroyed. And if the glory of that weren't enough, he had an ace up his sleeve that he would play and then relish and relive for the rest of his days. His one regret was that Johann would never learn of that final coup; perhaps he should tell him before he had him killed. Yes. Imagine the look on Johann's face when he learned that one of the people who had destroyed his family line was his very own son.

~~~~~~~~~~~~~~~~

While the Sparrow happily wended his way toward Edinburgh, Skye caught up with Taryn and informed him of all that she knew. As Taryn listened to his faithful ally, he realized that he would have to get his hands on the sword and remove its spell if he were ever to defeat Carlson and the rest of Lord Royce's men. As he and Skye perused the perimeter of the enemy camp and discovered the location of Carlson's tent, he began to hatch his plan. He would fill Julia in when they spoke tonight, and then he would steal in and get the sword. Taryn could feel his anticipation and power building as he made plans for the mission of stealth that lay ahead of him.

Chapter Ten

The sun, which the Stag and his companion had enjoyed, was also shining brightly over the castle as Julia arose and began preparing for the day's journey. Cook had packed lots of goodies which the trio would share with Sarah, the woman who would begin Thomas's training in plant medicine. Julia had trained under Sarah herself and found the woman to be loving and knowledgeable, a perfect combination for a first teacher for Thomas.

Nanny Margret, who had cared for Julia and Taryn when they were young, would accompany them to Sarah's. Because of Nanny's advanced age, Julia had arranged for her to travel in the relative comfort of a carriage while Julia would ride her faithful steed, Firefly. The trio would stay on for a few weeks' lessons with Sarah, during which time Julia hoped to hone and deepen her own spellwork. All too often these days, the only magic that she was able to practice was that which was required to keep them all safe on a daily basis. Although she didn't disparage the worth of those skills, she found that she missed being a student and learning about some of the newer teachings.

After checking that Nanny and Thomas were up and preparing to depart, Julia set about finding her father for a brief farewell. She found him studying land maps and strategizing with some of his advisors in a large room off of the dining hall. "Good morning, Father."

"Ah, good morning, Child." Johann looked up distractedly but brightened when he saw his only daughter's face. "What are you up to today?"

"Nanny leaves to visit her friend in the country. I thought that Thomas and I would take a short ride just into the woods to see her off. We won't go far."

Johann struggled with this information. He knew that telling Julia that she couldn't do something was useless, but he worried about her taking the boy off of the premises. Had he known that Julia was taking the boy farther off the premises than he had ever been before, Johann would surely have put a stop to that. That was one of the main reasons that Julia didn't tell him of her plans. The other was that because they were currently at war, it seemed prudent to keep their destination known to as few people as possible.

Julia considered her father somewhat naive about people. He believed that all of his men could be trusted. Julia was more wary. Even the coachmen didn't know their exact destination. Only Nanny, Taryn, and Julia knew the full plans. And, of course, Sarah who had been corresponding with Julia for the past few weeks via Julia's ally the Rook. Poor bird. Between flying over Royce's army to ferret out their plans and bearing missives between Julia and Sarah, she was certainly earning her keep. Julia reminded herself that she would have to reward her. Maybe a special hunting foray near Sarah's. The forests out that way were full of small game.

After taking her father's leave, Julia hurried to collect the camping supplies that she and Thomas would need for their overnight forest stay. Then she went to check on the horses and finally, midway through the morning, to fetch Nanny and Thomas. The boy was so excited by this time that he could barely stand still.

"Julia. Julia. Can I bring my bow and arrows?"

"Of course, Thomas. We will need you to defend us as we cross the forest."

The boy's eyes widened as he thought seriously about this new responsibility. "I would never let anything happen to you or Nanny, Julia."

"I know that, TomCat, and I feel perfectly safe with you by my side." She turned to the woman standing beside her nephew. "Is everything ready, Nanny?"

"All set. I will pick up the basket from Cook, and Thomas and I will follow behind you shortly."

"Please have the coachman pick up the camping supplies in my room and bring those, as well."

Nanny tilted her head and looked at Julia. "Camping supplies? Why do we need those?"

"I have decided that Thomas and I will stay in the forest this evening. We'll meet you in Settler's Woods after breakfast tomorrow morning and then all proceed together to Sarah's."

44

Nanny's brow creased as she worried about her young charge. "Are you sure that's safe, Julia?"

"Nanny, you know that I would never make a choice that I felt was unsafe for Thomas." She gently touched the older woman on the arm. "Don't worry. We'll have plenty of protection around us."

"Well, if you're sure..." Nanny also knew that it was useless to argue with Julia once her mind was made up. At least Thomas would ride in the safety of the carriage. "Will you pick Thomas up at the inn?"

"I thought that Thomas could ride with me if he would like."

"Oh yes, Julia. Yes!"

Despite Thomas' enthusiastic response, Nanny was still about to protest when Julia added, "My father is expecting Thomas and I to see you off. He will have to be on Firefly with me." That effectively ended any further debate that Nanny might have mustered and she sighed in frustration and departed to retrieve the basket from Cook in the kitchen.

Julia, who was smiling as she listened to Nanny's muttering which faded with her retreat, turned to Thomas, ruffled his hair, and said, "We're all set, Thomas. Let's go!"

Chapter Eleven

Several moments later, Julia and Thomas joined Julia's horse, Firefly, down in the castle courtyard. Much to the dismay of the stable boy, the steed had been impatiently prancing about while waiting for his mistress to arrive. The grateful youth was only too happy to turn over control of the spirited animal to Julia who calmed him with a few softly spoken words.

Firefly wasn't the only one filled with exuberance on this bright fall morning. The courtyard was also alive with visitors and local village folk who were running errands or just enjoying the fine weather. Many of them called out a greeting to Julia and Thomas as they passed by, and a few stopped to share the latest news or chat for a moment.

For as long as Julia could remember, the castle courtyard had always been a place of gathering and activity. Local folk and merchants from all over came here at different times of the year to sell their wares, and there were often brightly dressed storytellers and performers who would entertain the crowd in order to win a coin or bit of food from the pleased audience.

Presiding over all of this color and activity was the gray stone castle that Johann and the family called home. It had an imposing, austere presence that belied the warmth that was accorded to all visitors when they arrived.

The front of the castle housed the common rooms such as the dining hall and Johann's office. All of these rooms opened onto a large balcony which stood a level above the courtyard and ran from one side of the castle to the other. On a clear day, a rider could be spotted miles away from this open space and Julia had often stood there watching for the return of her brother or father when they were out on business.

To the rear of the castle and another floor up were the family sleeping quarters. These rooms were away from the noise of the courtyard and afforded stunning views of the valley and the river which led to the ocean a bit farther off. They also had balconies, although each was private and they weren't interconnected.

The entire castle and courtyard were perched atop a long hill which was sufficiently steep to discourage quick access, and yet not so steep as to prevent approach. This location was considered one of the best in all of Scotland as it afforded sweeping panoramas of the countryside and prevented a stealthy approach. Further discouragement from attack was presented by the high castle walls and sturdy drawbridge which ensconced the courtyard.

The drawbridge was currently open and would remain so until sunset this evening when it would close until the following day's sunrise. Unless they could manage to rouse the guard, anyone who was outside the walls at sunset would remain there until the next morning. Anyone, that is, except a select few.

As children, Taryn and Julia had been caught outside of the walls after hours and had to ask the guard to lower the drawbridge. The guard had reported the incident to Johann the next morning, and the children had suffered his anger and subsequent punishment. Even though they knew that his anger was driven by fear for their safety, they were determined to avoid his wrath in the future and still maintain their freedom; therefore, they quickly discovered an alternate means of entry onto the castle grounds.

Far below and tucked off to the right side of the castle was a door which led to the dungeon area. It was the very door that Julia had accessed yesterday when she sought out Stephen in the stables. The door was hidden behind some bushes and was only known by a few of the guards and some unfortunate prisoners. Long ago, a set of keys had gone missing from one of the guards and had never been found. Since that time, Julia and Taryn had gratefully employed said keys and this hidden entrance on numerous occasions.

Once inside the area near the dungeon, they could access the upper floors through a series of tunnels and thus return to their rooms undetected. Although this strategy worked well for Taryn and Julia, sometimes they were accompanied by those whom it didn't suit at all. The tunnels were dark and narrow, and experience had shown that navigating them with the horses was a bit tricky. It may be only a short distance from the dungeon area to the stables, but even so, Julia and Taryn had to use all of their powers of persuasion to lead the nervous animals through them.

Both Julia and Firefly were just as happy that this morning's trip didn't require the use of the passage through the dungeons. Today's subterfuge lay more in the secrecy of their destination. It was a deception that caused some lingering guilt when Julia looked up to see her father standing on the balcony waiting to see her and Thomas off on their "brief ride." She hated to deceive the man, but she could think of no other way to assure their safety so well as secrecy.

Before she could linger too long with her thoughts, she was pulled out of her reverie by Thomas who had also spotted Johann standing by the parapet.

"Look, Julia. It's Grandfather." Thomas shouted to his grandfather as he waved happily. "He came to say good-bye."

"Yes, he did." Julia waved to her father and turned to strap the last of their saddlebags into place. Just as she finished, she heard the cry of the Rook who was circling above the castle.

Thomas looked up and pointed. "Over there, Julia. It's Reggie."

Julia responded offhandedly. "I see her, Thomas. She's calling good morning to us."

Thomas looked confused by his aunt's misunderstanding and said, "No, she's not. She's telling you that the Wolf is waiting by the stream."

Julia, who was brought up short by her nephew's words, stopped what she was doing and looked at him in shock. Indeed, that was exactly what Reggie had said. When had the boy started to understand the animals? Most enchanters could understand the meaning behind the cries of their own allies, but precious few could understand the cries of other animals. This was incredible.

Julia realized that she would have to be more careful around Thomas until she determined whether he could hear the mindlink between her and the Rook as well as he understood the Rook's cries.

With a surface calm, Julia replied, "Why indeed you're right, Thomas." She realized that Thomas may be worried that a Wolf would be waiting for them by the outskirts of the castle grounds. In an effort to allay any fear he might have, she said, "I hope you know that you don't have to be scared of the Wolf. She's an ally of mine, just as Tiger is for you."

"Does that mean that Wolf is an ally of mine, too?"

"Not exactly. My Wolf works with me, but because she knows how much I love you, she'll work to take care of you, as well. You can always trust my Wolf. She wants to help me, and she knows that by helping protect you, she helps me, too."

"Will we be in danger?"

She lifted him onto the saddle as she thought about how to reply. "Well Thomas, you know that these are difficult times. Your father is at war fighting Royce's army. That means that there are people who don't have our best interests at heart." She paused, hoping that she hadn't said too much. "We just have to be careful. That's all. Nothing will happen to you while I'm around. You can count on that." With that, Julia pulled herself into the saddle and gave orders for the coachmen to follow with Nanny Margret as soon as she was ready.

As they began the ride through the courtyard, Julia asked her young charge the question that was foremost on her mind. "Hey, TomCat, how long have you understood the Rook?"

"I dunno. Doesn't everybody? She does speak clearly you know."

She laughed fondly at his typical straightforward reply. Sometimes he was so like his father. "I know. But most people can't understand animals."

"Why?"

She smiled at the innocent question. "I don't know. But it's a gift that you have. I think for now it should be our secret. Okay?"

"Okay, but can I tell Father when he comes home?"

"Of course. It'll be a great surprise for him." Julia smiled as she thought of Taryn's delight at the forthcoming news. His son was quickly proving his abilities in several areas, particularly the nature-based healing arts. Working with animals

49

was one of a Druid's strengths and Thomas had a decided advantage in being able to understand them. Perhaps this was his future. Only time would tell, but Julia knew that her nephew had enormous potential. She was happy that she could be here to witness its coming to fruition.

As Firefly crossed over the drawbridge, Julia and Thomas both turned to wave good-bye to Johann. Once they turned back and started down the steep hill, Julia automatically focused her thoughts on the trip ahead of them. In order to travel to Sarah's, they would first cross through the small forest that lay at the edge of the castle grounds. Then they would travel northwest for several hours around the river inlet. Finally they would enter Settler's Woods, a large forest where they would camp for the night. The next morning, they would have only a few more hours to ride before they reached the far edge of the woods and the beginning of Sarah's property.

As Firefly crossed the small bridge over the stream and entered the forest, Julia once again appreciated how beautiful her home was. The castle stood high on a hill overlooking a fertile valley, a small forest with a river inlet running beside it, and a few hours ride to the east, the ocean's edge.

For as long as Julia remembered, she and Taryn had enjoyed playing and working on the grounds and in the tiny forest nearby. Indeed, she and Taryn knew every possible hiding place and every animal that lived in these woods and were as comfortable in them as they were in the castle - sometimes even more so.

As Firefly headed toward the edge of the forest, Julia reached out with her mind and linked with the Wolf and her pack.

We're here, Julia. Up ahead by the rock to your left.

She scanned in the direction indicated. A sudden movement caught her eye. *I see you. Thank you for coming with us on this journey.*

It's a good chance for us to do some hunting, train the cubs, and explore some new territory, too.

Please be careful. Watch out for the coachmen, and don't let them glimpse you this time.

Don't worry. That lesson was learned the hard way by one of our over-eager cubs. It won't happen again.

Good. I don't want anything happening to any of you.

We're going to scout ahead. Let me know if you need me.

All right. Thanks.

Julia glanced at Thomas who was happily looking around at the forest and all of its wonders. He didn't seem to have heard the mindlink between her and the Wolf, but she would have to be careful until she was absolutely sure. She didn't want to frighten the child unnecessarily. He already had so much to deal with in his young life; his mother had died, and his father was away fighting a war. It was more than enough for anyone to handle, let alone a five-year-old. Still, he was so mature in many ways. And his abilities were amazing. Who knew where they would lead? She could hardly wait to see.

Chapter Twelve

After a leisurely day of riding, they finally reached Settler's Woods in the late afternoon and neared the spot where Julia planned to stay overnight with Thomas. It was a place that she and Taryn had camped before, and she knew it well. It was hidden and private and wouldn't be seen by anyone, even with the fire that Julia was about to build. It also held a special surprise which was sure to delight her nephew.

When they reached the small clearing, Julia pulled Firefly to a stop by a rambling stream. "Okay, Thomas, we'll sleep here for the night. Let's unpack Firefly and get things set up as much as we can while we wait for Nanny and the supplies."

The wolves joined them as they gathered wood, and Julia was not surprised to look up and see Thomas playing with some of the young cubs. After she had finished stacking the wood and settling in, Julia turned to her young charge and asked, "Shall we take a walk and look around?"

"Yes! Can the wolves come with us?"

"I think it would be best if they stayed behind. The other animals will run and hide if the wolves are around."

Thomas turned to the wolf cubs and explained where he was going. As if they understood, the cubs scurried off to join the rest of the pack who were crossing the stream to scavenge for dinner.

We'll be here if you need us, Julia.

Thanks, Wolf. We'll be back soon.

As Julia led Thomas through the forest, she pointed out the different trees and the tracks of the animals. Thomas, once again, proved to be a quick study and spotted some of the small animals before Julia did. He even spied a little sparrow that had followed them on their walk and was perched on a nearby tree.

"I think he likes us, Aunt Julia. He's following us."

Julia eyed the tiny bird. "What makes you think that?"

"I saw him at the castle the other day, and now he's here with us."

Julia, thinking that her nephew had an overactive imagination, said, "I doubt that he's the same sparrow. They don't usually travel this far alone."

Thomas tilted his head in the way that he did when he was about to become insistent and said, "It **is** the same one, Julia. I know it is."

Weeks later, Julia was to reflect that if she had taken Thomas more seriously and remembered her earlier musings on how skilled he was with animals, she might not have dismissed his words so readily. Unfortunately, it was only in hindsight that she recognized this moment for the early warning that it was.

With the Sparrow already forgotten, Julia turned to her nephew and asked a question that she already knew the answer to. "Thomas, do you want me to show you where the fairies live?"

His eyes lit up. "Real fairies?"

Julia laughed. "Well, of course, real fairies. What other kind are there?"

"Oh boy!"

"Okay, but first I must tell you that there are certain rules to visiting with fairies."

Thomas gave his aunt a puzzled look. "What kind of rules?"

"Well, fairies are very sensitive, so you always want to approach them with a lot of respect. If they show themselves to you, it's a gift and you must honor that gift. It's very rare for the fairies to choose to befriend a human. Ready?"

He nodded and whispered in excitement. "Ready." Together they quietly walked toward a grassy knoll where Julia knew a group of fairies lived and worked. They had been kind to her and Taryn in the past, and she hoped that they would share that kindness with her nephew. As they approached the area, she could feel the energy in the air.

"Do you feel that energy shift, Thomas?"

Thomas looked at her with wide eyes, cocked his head, and stayed motionless for a moment. Then he turned to his aunt and said, "Yes. It feels…special - like my birthday."

"Hmm. I never thought of it that way before, but that makes sense. Whenever you feel that energy, there's magic around. You just need to take a moment to notice."

He nodded his small head solemnly, then smiled and said, "Look, Julia. The fairies are there."

Julia looked in the direction of the young child's finger and noticed several fairies dancing from plant to plant. They were collecting roots and seeds from the stalks and putting them into small baskets. At first they appeared to be just flashes of light, but when you looked more closely, you could see distinct individuals. Thomas whispered, "Oh Julia, they're so beautiful." As if pleased by the young child's accolades, one of the fairies turned to Thomas, curtsied and laid down a small plant.

Julia immediately recognized the gesture. "Look, Thomas, they're giving you a gift."

"For me?"

The fairy nodded her head and hopped off to another plant.

"You should be honored that the fairies gave you this plant, Thomas. It's important to acknowledge this gift with a gift in return." Julia knew that this next gesture should come from Thomas, so she asked, "How will you thank them?"

Thomas immediately reached for the small bag that he had hung off of a rope tied around his waist and began to rustle through it. In it were all of the treasures that little boys collect in their travels. Finally, he withdrew a beautiful seashell that he and his father had found during a trip to the shore. He held it up to show Julia. "I will give them this shell because they can hear the ocean in it." He pressed the shell to his aunt's ear for a moment. "Father says it's like music, and I think the fairies will like it." Thomas gently moved toward the fairy knoll and placed the shell on the ground. He bent to retrieve the plant that the fairies had given him and whispered, "Thank you." Then after showing the plant to Julia, he carefully placed it in his bag. As they walked back to camp after wishing the wee folk well, Thomas asked, "Why were they collecting plants?"

"The fairies use plants for medicine, just like we do. They're very skilled at knowing which plants to use. After you work with Sarah for a while, you'll know which plants to use to help cure people, too."

"Which plant did they give me, Julia?"

"We'll have to ask Sarah to be sure but I think that they gave you Fairyweed which is used to cure cuts and scrapes and take away the pain."

"I like the fairies, Julia. Can we visit them again?"

"I think the fairies like you, too. I'm sure that they would be happy to see you again. We'll stop in on our way back to the castle." Suddenly, she felt the presence of the Wolf in her mind.

The carriage approaches. All is well. They're stopping to leave the camping supplies.

Thank you, Wolf. Other than the carriage, is the forest clear?

Yes. We have scouts posted and all is clear.

Excellent. Thomas and I will be back at the campsite shortly and will stay there for the evening. Taryn should be checking in soon.

Fine. We'll let you know if there is any danger. Some of the cubs want to sleep by Thomas if that's all right. I'll come and join you after I check all of the outposts.

That'll be fine. I'll see you later. Thank you.

Chapter Thirteen

Back at the army camp, Taryn could feel his heart racing and his blood pumping as he began his final preparations for the evening's mission. He had spoken with Julia and Thomas earlier, and his sister would be expecting the sword at Sarah's house when she arrived tomorrow afternoon. If Taryn knew his sister at all, he also knew that she would be performing all sorts of protection spells to assure his safety during his activities this evening.

His plan was simple and direct, which was typical of him. He would sneak in to the enemy camp and steal the enchanted sword, replacing it with an identical copy. At the edge of the forest, his fastest rider would be waiting. When Taryn had the sword in his possession, he would give it to the rider who would bring it swiftly to Sarah's cottage.

Then Julia, who had the stronger spell working skills of the siblings, would remove the enchantment. This would be the trickiest part of the endeavor, as the spell must have been placed on the sword by an extremely powerful sorcerer. When Julia was done, Taryn would return the original sword and remove the duplicate. To all eyes, the original would appear the same, but there would be one crucial difference: it would no longer be enchanted.

As Taryn gathered the herbs and powders that he needed for his spell work, Gern approached him carrying a simple silver sword.

"Here it is, Taryn. We found the plainest sword made of fine silver, although I don't understand why it needed to have no ornamentation."

"I'm going to place a cloaking spell on the sword so that it appears to be the enchanted sword. Since we don't have time to physically recreate the exact sword with all of its engravings, the spell works best when the replacement is plain with no carving different from the original."

"Why don't we just leave the replacement there? Why do we have to return the original if this will look the same?"

"Because the cloaking spell will only last 48 hours at most. It's imperative that we return the original as soon as possible."

"Well, let's get going then."

Taryn looked at Gern and shook his head. "I appreciate your willingness to come with me Gern, but I have to do this alone." Seeing the man's crestfallen face, he added, "It'll be safer for me. I can shapeshift if need be, but you can't. If you were with me, we might both be discovered."

"I'm coming with you. I have to." Gern's note of desperation alerted Taryn to the man's subtext. He decided that it was time to clear the air once and for all. Gern may be 6'4" and built like a warrior, but Taryn knew that it was someone a lot smaller who had him quaking in his boots. He looked fondly at the bearded man with shaggy brown hair. Once again, he decided to be straightforward and cut to the heart of the matter.

"Look Gern, I know that my sister sent you to watch over me." Gern started to shake his head when Taryn interrupted. "Don't try to deny it; it would be a waste of our time. I don't mind. Really, I don't." Taryn patted the man's shoulder. "You've been a fine officer and friend. I couldn't have chosen better myself. That's why I never said anything."

Gern looked at the ground and mumbled something about letting Julia down. Taryn couldn't help feeling sorry for the poor man, as he knew Julia's wrath when piqued and suspected that Gern did as well. He decided to take pity on him and offer a compromise. "I'll tell you what Gern, you can wait with Drew and ride back to camp with me after he leaves for Sarah's with the sword."

Immediately, his officer looked up and the relief on his face was palpable. "Well, what are we waiting for then?"

Taryn laughed out loud at Gern's obvious pleasure in being included. "All right, Gern. Give me an hour or so to prepare the sword and we'll be off."

"I'll see to the horses and wait with Drew."

"Excellent." With that, Taryn turned to the business at hand and began to work his magic. He used the herbs and ointments he had gathered to coat the sword and then he placed it into the campfire while he recited the magical words which would seal the cloaking spell in place. He had done his preparation earlier in the day and contacted his teacher for the correct spell to do the job. There was no time to waste this evening.

When he was done, he quenched the fire and removed the sword. It still looked like a plain silver sword to him, but he knew that it would appear exactly like the enchanted sword to everyone else. He carefully wrapped it in a piece of leather, grabbed his cloak, and hurried off to meet Gern and Drew.

~~~~~~~~~~~~~~~

The trio journeyed quickly and quietly to the British camp. When they arrived at the outer perimeter, they found an area where Drew and Gern could safely wait. Much to his dismay, Gern could not get Taryn to revoke his earlier decision to enter the camp alone. He watched as the man whom he had been assigned to watch and who now felt more like his brother than his employer made his final preparations.

Taryn blackened his face and placed a dark cloak around his body. During his final moments before heading off, he said the magical words of the Deer and silently placed the spell of invisibility on himself. As he started to walk away, Gern would have sworn that Taryn disappeared into the tree line.

Chapter Fourteen

Once away from Gern's watchful eyes, Taryn leaned against a tree and took several deep breaths intended to slow his pulse and calm his breathing. He needed to be steady as he entered the hub of the enemy camp. He was loathe to admit that there were other reasons for his caution, but truth be told, he was still suffering some ill effects from the poison.

Although the physical wound was healing nicely, Taryn was fighting waves of dizziness and nausea which did not seem to be abating. If anything, they were increasing in frequency and were particularly present when his adrenaline was flowing, just as it was now. He had been trying numerous elixirs designed to re-stabilize his blood, but nothing seemed to be working. He would feel better for a few hours, then would suffer another setback. He realized that he should probably consult with Julia, but he didn't want to add to her worries. He was counting on his body to overcome this, if he gave it some time.

As soon as he was steady, he pushed those thoughts to the side. It wasn't important now; he would deal with it later. For now, there was only one object in his sights: the enchanted sword.

If Skye's information were correct, the sword had been cast with a spell that made it the ultimate weapon. In the hands of a warrior, such as the British Captain Carlson, it acted as both protector and destroyer. First of all, the steel was reinforced with magic, making it almost impossible to shatter. This allowed for the sword to act as a shield blocking blows from other swords without causing itself harm. Secondly, the ruby in the hilt of the sword was cut and programmed to affect anyone who stared at it for a while. According to Skye, who had witnessed a practice session with the sword, the opponent would become mesmerized and his rhythms in the fight would be slowed and ultimately compromised, making the sword a mighty weapon for a well-trained warrior.

Taryn wended his way across the British camp, careful to avoid any twigs that might snap and alert the enemy to his presence. Even with the cloak of invisibility, he still needed to use caution. Thanks to earlier recognizance, his course was sure and took him directly toward the Captain's tent where he knew the sword to be.

Once there, he listened at the back of the tent for any noise which would indicate Carlson's presence and whether he was sleeping or awake. Hearing only a steady, rhythmic breathing, Taryn lifted the back corner of the tent and slid under it as quietly as he could. Inside, he took a moment to acclimate himself to the layout and let his eyes adjust to the absence of moonlight. Once that was done, he quickly spied the sleeping figure of the Captain on the far side of the tent.

The sword was not as readily visible as the man; however, Taryn had expected this and was prepared. He tuned in to his inner knowing and searched for any energy sources in the room. He was immediately drawn to a pile of clothes in the far corner. He could almost feel a pulse beneath the pile. Silently Taryn gave the Captain credit for hiding the sword in an unexpected place, and avoiding the all too obvious trunk which sat in the center of the space. After locating the sword, he scanned the area for any possible traps that might have been laid. Sensing only a trip wire in the tent entrance and some sort of spring device on the trunk, Taryn crept toward the pile of clothes with the replacement sword by his side.

Slowly, he removed the clothing in the precise order in which it had been laid. At the bottom of the pile was an old piece of material with something inside of it. Reverently, Taryn ran his hands about two inches over the piece of material. He could feel the sword's power pulsing. This enchantment was strong, so much so that Taryn hesitated to unwrap the sword for fear that it might emit a glow in the darkened space. Not wanting to waste too much time analyzing the situation, he decided to go with his first instinct and perform the switch as quickly as possible. He lined up the two bundles and unwrapped the duplicate sword so that it would be ready for the switch. His pulse was racing and he took a moment to steady his hands.

Quickly, Taryn unwrapped the magnificent sword, replaced it with the duplicate, and rewrapped the empowered version in his own leather scrap. Even though the sword was exposed for only a few seconds, its unwrapped energy was enough to disturb Carlson's sleep. Taryn froze as the Captain mumbled and rolled over. He was now turned and facing Taryn. If his eyes opened, he would spot him immediately. Taryn remained still, looked at the ground and calmed his breathing as much as he could. He went deep inside himself, knowing that if he were to look at Carlson or move, he might awaken the man from the very shallow sleep state he was in.

After several tense minutes, Carlson stopped mumbling and settled back into a deeper state of sleep. Taryn waited a while longer to be sure and then he began to reassemble the clothing pile in the exact order in which it had previously appeared. He didn't know how meticulous this captain was about details, but he wasn't taking any chances that he didn't have to. He would never forgive himself if something as simple as a pile of clothing ruined all of his stealth and preparation.

As Taryn worked, he mused on the time that he had tried to hide in his sister's room and scare her when they were children. He had heedlessly moved some of her belongings in order to climb into the large trunk at the foot of her bed. Upon entering her room, Julia immediately noticed the misplaced belongings and, suspecting the truth, had placed as much weight on the trunk as she could, thereby neatly trapping her brother inside. She had let him stew in there all through supper and then feigned surprise when she opened the trunk to fetch her nightgown and found her brother stowed away in there.

Taryn had learned that lesson well and carefully placed the Captain's clothing back in its original order. Once finished, he went to the corner of the tent and was about to exit when he was alerted by a noise outside. He settled in to wait until he could decipher its course of direction and cause.

Taryn knew that he hadn't been entirely honest with Gern in the earlier discussion about shapeshifting. It was true that he was skilled at shifting his forms, but what Gern didn't know was that if forced to shift, Taryn would also be forced to leave the sword behind. He couldn't shapeshift and still hold onto the sword. If he left the sword behind, the plan would be discovered and thwarted. Two swords that appeared alike would fool no one in the camp. Even though Taryn would most likely get out alive, they would still be faced with the problem of the sword and its enchantment, as well as intensified surveillance and patrols. Taryn was determined to prevent this and waited patiently.

His patience was soon rewarded as the source of the noise approached. Two of Carlson's men who were on patrol were chatting quietly, and as they neared the Captain's tent, Taryn became privy to the conversation and its tenor. He noted with satisfaction that they hadn't discovered either of his waiting cohorts as the conversation was clearly casual in nature. After a few moments, the men moved on and before long, Taryn was able to escape the tent and make his way safely back to his allies.

Chapter Fifteen

When Taryn removed the invisibility spell and suddenly appeared before his men, he thought that the startled Gern might accidentally stab him. Luckily, Gern quickly identified his leader, grabbed him in an exuberant, and somewhat awkward, hug of relief, and uttered a refrain of "Well, I'll be damned."

"Good grief, Gern." Taryn squirmed in the man's grasp. "You seem positively surprised and delighted to see me. Am I to take it that you didn't think I'd succeed?"

Gern, only just realizing that he was holding Taryn airborne in a hug, blinked in shock and roughly deposited his leader back on the ground. "No, sir. I never thought that at all. I'm just ... uh..."

Taryn laughed quietly and changed the subject. "Let's see the prize that all of this fuss was about. Shall we?" Slowly he unwrapped the sword. All three men stared spellbound in appreciation of its beauty and power. The sword had a magnificent dragon engraved down its length and culminating at its handle. The dragon had a ruby for an eye which was located right on the hilt of the sword. They stared reverently, not only in appreciation of the fine workmanship, but also of the soft glow of power which was apparent in the moonlight. All too soon, Taryn broke the spell and rewrapped the sword, handing it to the rider.

"We'd best get you on your way now before I'm tempted to keep this sword for myself. Are you sure of the route you will take?"

"Yes, sir."

"The Hawk will go with you and warn you of any traps that lie in waiting or men that are set on your trail."

"Fine, sir. Where will she meet me?"

Taryn's eyes glittered with amusement. "She's been here all along. Haven't you noticed?" With that he pointed to the silent bird of prey sitting quietly in a tree above them. He lifted his arm and she settled quickly on the proffered perch. "This is Skye. She will see you safely to Sarah's and then fly back directly to me to report on your successful arrival. It will be up to you to make your own way back. Can you handle that Drew?"

"I'm sure that I can, sir."

"So am I. That's why I've chosen you for this important journey. Ride well."

"Thank you, sir."

~~~~~~~~~~~~~~~~

Taryn and Gern watched as the man and Hawk went safely off and then started back to camp. It was a leisurely ride, and once out of earshot of the British camp, the two men conversed in the easy manner which had been a hallmark of their recently developing friendship. In fact, had Taryn met Gern before Julia, he might just as readily have hired the man as she had.

Gern had been in the Edinburgh area only a short while when he met Julia on one of her trips to help a local family who needed healing work. Gern had moved there after losing both of his parents to illness and his small farm to debt. Being an only child, he'd had no reason to stay in his small village in the southwestern part of Scotland and had traveled east to Edinburgh, a more populated and, he hoped, less lonely part of the world.

The local farmers had immediately recognized Gern's superior strength, willingness to work and general good nature. He had been working for several of them and sleeping in their barns for a few months when he met Julia.

As soon as the war began and it was decided that Taryn would lead the army, Julia had contacted Gern and hired him to shadow and protect her brother. Gern's strength had assured him of a post in the army and his devotion and willingness to do whatever was needed had quickly brought him to Taryn's notice. In a short time, the two men had become friends just as Julia had hoped they would.

It was a testament to this friendship that Taryn had not removed Gern from his duties once he had discovered the man's hidden agenda for serving in the army. Indeed, he was as fond of Gern as if the two men had been allies for years. In addition, if he removed Gern from his post, Julia would just send someone else, and Taryn might not be as fond of the replacement. So all in all, the current arrangement suited everyone. Taryn was just happy that it was now in the open, and he and Gern no longer had to pretend.

After they returned to camp, Taryn, who was feeling good about the evening's work, still had plenty of energy coursing through him. He decided to use that energy to take a short flight and inspect the perimeters of both his and the British camps.

After bidding Gern a good night, he walked to a sheltered area behind the camp and began the process of shapeshifting into a hawk. Once the transformation was complete, he took to the air and spread his wings. This was what he loved the most about being an enchanter: the freedom and ease of flying as a hawk or running as a deer and the adventure of stealing the sword. He thought wistfully of all the childhood hours he had spent just stretching his wings or planning coup on his sister. He didn't get to do any of those things often any more, so he was darn well going to enjoy them while he could.

As he flew, he formed lazy arcs and spirals while slowly making his way around the camp. Seeing that all was well, he headed off toward the British settlement. Once there, he inspected the enemy campsite and noted that it was also quiet and calm. Peace reigned. That was a very good sign. Surely if anyone had discovered the sword missing, there would be a ruckus occurring below. Satisfied, he decided to check the outer posts of the enemy camp and assure himself that their positions hadn't been changed. Knowing the placement of enemy guards was information that could prove quite useful in the future.

Another benefit of shapeshifting was enjoying the enhanced senses that his animal allies had. The sharp eyes of the hawk quickly spotted the British guard standing alone on the far outskirts of the camp. As Taryn approached this final outpost, he noticed that the young guard had been lulled into a sense of complacency by the late hour and quiet forest. Taryn's current duties as commander of the army had required a recent suppression of his normally exuberant sense of humor. He couldn't resist taking advantage of the moment which now presented itself, and he decided to have some fun at the guard's expense.

He launched himself into steep dive intended to take him close to the British soldier's head. Just as he closed in, he swerved and let out an ungodly squawk. The poor lad leapt into the air and shouted in alarm. Taryn chuckled to himself and thought that there was one soldier who would never relax on the post again - at least not for the rest of **this** evening.

As he flew away, Taryn pondered that there was something about the young guard that seemed familiar, but for the life of him, he couldn't figure out what it was. Finally, he just shrugged it off and continued on his flight. If it were important, it would come to him.

A short while later, he arrived in camp, tired but happy with the evening's work. He knew that Julia would be able to take care of the spell's removal. She had always been a whiz at potions and would clearly enjoy the challenge of besting another sorcerer and undoing his work. In fact, he may just as well consult her about the poison on the sword and be done with it once and for all.

As for Taryn, he just enjoyed the adventure. He could handle the potions and spells, but he preferred the action that he had partaken in this evening. As he shifted back into his human form, he realized that he was also looking forward to the adventure that lay ahead of him when he had to return the sword to its rightful owner.

Although he never liked to over-think a plan, he couldn't resist a bit of strategizing as to how he would return the sword. Some of his enjoyment lay in the scheming required to devise a simple, foolproof plan. Who knew that war could be so much fun?

Chapter Sixteen

Julia was awakened by something rough which touched her face when she rolled over. It was piece of bark that had fallen by her ear. She threw it to the side and slowly roused herself from the deep sleep she almost always experienced in nature. The early morning forest was alive with sounds all around her. Birds were singing, the brook was gurgling, and Firefly was munching on some nearby greenery. It was only slowly that it came to her that there was a sound missing. Thomas must still be sleeping soundly a few feet away. She could see the mound of bedclothes from where she was.

It was time to get up and prepare for the final leg of the journey to Sarah's. She would have to rouse her sleepy nephew as well, but first she would find some berries for them to enjoy for breakfast. As Julia got up, she noticed that Reggie and the wolf pack were absent from the camp. They had probably gone to fetch their own breakfast. No matter. They would all reunite shortly.

Julia packed her gear and got everything ready for the carriage to pick up. She picked some berries from a nearby bush and went to rouse her nephew. He must really be in a deep sleep if he hadn't heard her packing up. "Okay sleepyhead, it's time to...Thomas?" He wasn't inside the mound of blankets which Julia had mistaken for his tiny body. She looked around. "Thomas? Where are you?"

Julia took a moment to tap in. Perhaps he had just ventured a short way; he knew better than to go too far. As soon as Julia tried to sense her nephew, her calm demeanor evaporated. She couldn't get much, but what she did get, she didn't like. She had a sense of fear around Thomas. That was all though. No clear picture, just darkness all around. Even as she began to act, searching the camp and its environs and calling his name, she recalled Taryn's dream. Thomas taken or lost. She prayed with all her heart that this wasn't happening now.

Julia raced down the small steam frightened that her nephew may have fallen in. As she ran shouting his name, she called to Reggie and the Wolf and told them what had happened. Neither had seen Thomas but both would return to camp immediately.

I'll never forgive any of us if Thomas is hurt.

Julia, calm down. He is most likely fine. You said yourself he was frightened, but you couldn't sense more.

The Wolf added, **He most likely wandered off. We'll go back to camp and pick up the trail from there.**

I'll fly over the fairy bower and see if he's gone there.

Good thinking both of you. I'm sorry I snapped. I'm so worried I can't think. Thank God I have you.

We'll find him, Julia.

Reggie, I almost forgot to tell you. He understands your cries so be sure to call to him as you search.

I will.

We'll try calling out, too.

Soon the forest was filled with wolf howls, bird cries and Julia's voice as all of them searched for Thomas. Julia became more frantic as time passed and she covered the area around the campsite. Although it was no more than thirty minutes or so since she had discovered him missing, she was becoming less and less confident of this ending well. Surely he must hear them calling to him. Why didn't he answer? The logical response was that he couldn't.

Tears began to pool in her eyes as she began to widen her search towards the fairy bower. It didn't make sense. If someone had taken him, he would have called out. He was surrounded by wolves all night. No one could have gotten near.

Julia, we've found him. Bring rope.

Thank God. Julia raced back to the camp to get rope even as she asked. *How is he?*

He's fine. Just scared. A little scratched, but fine.

What happened?

It looks as if he fell down some sort of hole, perhaps an old cave or well.

She grabbed the rope and turned. As she was about to ask where they were, she saw the Wolf run in to the outskirts of camp.

This way. I left the pack with him.

As Julia followed the Wolf, tears of gratitude streamed down her face. *How did this happen?*

I think he was on the way to the fairy bower when he got lost. He's just a short way off the path you used yesterday.

But he looks fine?

Yes. He was holding his arm – it might be broken, but he'll be fine. He is frightened.

I bet he is. Why do five-year-olds have to be so damn independent?

Before the Wolf could remind Julia of her own youthful adventures, they arrived at the sight. "Thomas!" Julia threw herself to the ground between the wolves that were keeping guard. They were positioned all around the rim of the hole into which her nephew had fallen. It was only about eight feet down, but that must have seemed a long way to Thomas.

"Julia! Julia!" As soon as he saw his aunt, the tears began to fully flow. It was as if knowing that he was safe, he could recognize how truly frightened he was.

"It's all right, Thomas. We're going to get you out of there."

"Julia, my arm hurts."

She saw that he was cradling it. "I can see that. Is it a sharp pain?"

Thomas nodded. "When I move it."

"All right. Keep it as still as you can."

Thomas nodded.

Julia turned to the Wolf. *He won't be able to hold on to a rope with that arm. I'll have to go down.* She looked around. *I can tie the rope on that tree, go down, tie it around Thomas and send him up. Do you think that you and the Wolf pack can pull him up if I support him from the bottom?*

Of course we can. The problem is the arm. We don't want it to hit the side of the hole as we pull him up.

Reggie who had been mysteriously absent for the past several minutes flew in and landed beside Julia. **There's a fallen branch a short way off that should do the trick. If we brace his arm with it, it should help protect it.**

Perfect. While Reggie and the Wolf went to fetch the branch, Julia cut a small piece of the rope to secure the branch to Thomas's arm and then tied the rest of it to a large tree nearby. While she worked, she kept up a steady stream of chatter to keep Thomas calm. She explained what they had planned to do and how careful Thomas would have to be with his arm as he was pulled from the hole. When she had the rope secure, she went to the edge of the hole and peered down at her nephew who was resting on the ground. The Wolf joined her and placed the branch by her side. Julia looked at the branch.

This should work perfectly. She tied the rope around her waist securing the branch against her body. "Move to the other side, Thomas. I'm coming down."

"Careful, Julia."

"It's a little late for that."

Thomas hung his head. "I'm sorry."

She started her descent with several pairs of eyes watching closely. "We'll discuss this later. Right now it's time to get you out."

Even though Julia descended carefully, several bits of rock slid out from under her. The ground seemed to be crumbling in and Julia could see how Thomas had fallen through. There was some wood under her feet suggesting perhaps an old tunnel or hiding place that was long deserted. The wood had probably rotted and anything that it was supporting had given way.

Julia reached the ground safely and Thomas came into her arms. She gave him a kiss and a quick glance over. The arm didn't appear to be broken, but it was badly sprained. Sarah would be able to help with that. She quickly secured the arm with the branch and tied Thomas around the waist. "Now Thomas, hold the rope with your good arm and use your feet to walk up the wall. She held his small body in position and called to the wolf. *Ready.*

The wolf pack was lined up at intervals along the rope with Reggie keeping watch on Thomas from a nearby tree. Slowly the pack pulled on the rope, careful not to let their very sharp teeth cut through it. Thomas' steady progress was made slower when he was out of Julia's reach. Finally he made it to the top of the hole and the Wolf grabbed his tunic and pulled him over. Untying the rope was a bit more complicated with the injured arm, but Thomas got it done and sent it back to Julia. She climbed up and in no time at all joined her nephew who had collapsed on the ground above. The Wolves fell to the ground around them.

After Julia caught her breath she turned to her nephew, "Thomas, I just don't understand. What happened?"

"I was going to say good-bye to the fairies."

"Without telling me? You know better than that."

"I left a note, Julia."

She looked at him. "What note? You can barely write."

"I drew a picture of the fairies on bark and put it right beside you."

Julia remembered the bark which she had rolled over onto and tossed to the side.

"Still Thomas, you should have awakened me. You had us all very frightened."

"I know. I'm sorry."

"Don't let it happen again, young man."

"I won't. I promise."

"Good." She stood up and held her hand out to him. "Now let's go back to camp and see to that arm."

When Julia and Thomas arrived back at camp, he showed her the bark note and she agreed that he had tried to tell her where he went, although she reminded him that waking her and getting permission would have been the correct choice. They were examining his arm when Nanny rode into camp. It took some minutes to explain the morning's adventure to Nanny who was adamant that a dejected Thomas ride the rest of the way in the carriage. As this seemed a prudent precaution, Julia agreed. She also secretly felt that it would remind Thomas that there were consequences to his actions: he would neither say good- bye to the fairies nor ride the horse with Julia.

Shortly thereafter a somber but relieved group set out once again.

Chapter Seventeen

The rest of the journey to Sarah's passed without incident, and they arrived safely at the small cottage in the early afternoon. As they cleared the forest, the picture which greeted them seemed to be out of a storybook. The tiny home was perched several yards back from the tree line and had a small pond in the front yard. The border of the pond was surrounded by a variety of wild flowers and herbs. The rest of the yard was wide open and filled with sunshine. They had barely ridden out of the forest when the door opened and a short, rounded woman with a smiling face emerged to greet them. While Julia showed the coachmen to the stables, Sarah bustled Nanny and Thomas inside and set about making them feel welcome.

Thomas was immediately charmed by Sarah who fussed over his arm, treating it with a salve and designing a sling to keep it immobile. She also managed to give Thomas a pointed lecture about his actions while remaining loving and kind. Julia, who was exhausted from the morning's ordeal, was grateful for the woman's ministrations.

After Thomas had been tended to, Nanny and Sarah, who were old friends from the days when Sarah had trained Taryn and Julia, set about catching up on all the news, While they did, Julia explored the perimeter of the land and took all the necessary safety precautions. The Wolf and Rook accompanied her as she set off on foot.

I'm going to place a shield around the space to keep the cottage protected from prying eyes. You two and the pack will be able to cross into the perimeter, but no one else will cross through without our knowing.

What about the forest creatures? I'm sure that they come and go often, the Wolf noted.

Good point. I will allow for those who are regulars but not any others except you. We can't underestimate our enemy. They could send a familiar to spy just as I have done with you two on many occasions.

The Rook settled on a nearby boulder. **How long will we be staying?**

We'll stay for a bit less than a fortnight. By that time, Thomas should be well on his way in his studies and should be able to continue on his own for a while. In the meantime, I'll work on the sword.

Have you seen it yet?

No. Sarah has it put aside. I'll look at it this evening. Once I determine how strong the enchantment is, I can decide what has to be done. But before I get to that, I need to place a memory draught in the coachmen's ale. I want no one other than us to know where Thomas is staying.

Do you think that's wise? What if you need defending?

If I do my job well, we will be defended. Besides, we have you and the wolf pack. Between all of us, I'm sure that we'll be safe.

Together the trio made their way around the perimeter of the land. As they walked, Julia sprinkled a sweet herb on the ground that would form the barrier at the outskirts of Sarah's property. She had found an herb that would do no harm to humans and wouldn't appeal to the hungry forest creatures. If any broke through this barrier, Julia, the Wolf, and Rook would all immediately know. In addition, Julia took a minute to put a power shield over the small cottage to make it appear harmless and uninteresting to any who passed by. One could never be too careful about energy leaks occurring while a young magician and healer was being trained. And Julia herself would be doing some intense energy work around the sword that Royce's army captain, Carlson, carried. She definitely didn't want that work being observed or disrupted.

When Julia was convinced that she had done all that she could, she returned to the cottage. After a brief stop there, she walked over to the stables where the coachmen were settling the horses and unloading the carriage. They were delighted to hear that they were to stay in a nearby inn and await word from Julia. This meant they would have time to socialize with the locals and visit the merchants in the area. Not to mention that the maids were reportedly quite comely in this region. In addition to bringing this good news, Julia had also brought with her two mugs of ale to quench the thirst of these hard workers.

After the men finished their ale and headed on the path to the town, Julia found a quiet spot in the barn and connected with their minds. Thanks to the potion that she had placed into the cups of ale, they were now open to suggestion. She mentally transferred the thoughts that she wished the coachmen to retain of their recent past history.

You have been given a fortnight's holiday leave after a victorious battle against Royce's men. Your Lord was extremely pleased with the job you have done. You will stay at the local inn, have plenty of entertainment, and relax until you receive word to leave and rejoin the army.

Julia could feel her projected thoughts enter the minds of the men, but she had to make sure that her task was accomplished. There was too much at stake these days to allow any loose ends.

Reggie, are you there?

I am here in the forest hunting for my dinner.

Can you do me a favor, old friend? I need you to fly over the coachmen and be sure that their conversation is of an appropriate nature. If the spell worked, they will believe themselves on holiday from the army. Please be sure that their banter indicates this and let me know.

I'll go now.

Thank you.

Chapter Eighteen

After she had contacted the Rook, Julia hurried back to the small cottage, anxious to examine the sword before her nightly conversation with her brother in the firelink. When she entered, Thomas and Sarah had their heads bent over the plant that the fairies had given him while Nanny dozed lightly by the fire. Sarah was explaining the importance of the fairies and the gift of friendship which Thomas had received.

"Indeed Thomas, Julia was right. This plant is called Fairyweed because it has an almost magical way of drawing the pain out of any small cut. It will stop the itching that comes with healing. Tomorrow, I'll show you how to mash and apply it. It's a very good place for you to start in your schooling on herbs and plants. One thing that Julia might not have shared is that a gift of Fairyweed from the wee folk is a promise of friendship. Do not take this lightly, Thomas. The fairies may be small, but they are powerful allies. Did you leave them a token of your thanks?"

"Yes, Sarah. I left them a shell that Father and I found on the beach."

"Well that's a good start. We'll make them another gift while you're here and you may leave it on your return journey. How does that sound?"

"What will we make?"

"I don't know yet. Perhaps you can think about that while you wash up for dinner. Oh, and Thomas, I have something which your father sent for you."

"Really! What is it Sarah?"

Sarah went to the shelf above the hearth and found a small, leather-bound, handwritten journal which she handed to the boy. It had twigs and plants sticking out all over it, and Julia recognized it immediately. "It's your father's notebook from when I taught him. In it you will find drawings and samples of all of the plants which we will be studying."

Thomas took the small book gently from Sarah's hands and looked at it with reverence. "You knew my father when he was little?"

Sarah smiled and said, "Not quite as little as you, but yes, your father and aunt were both students of mine at one time."

Thomas nodded his head very solemnly. "That must mean you are very old."

Julia laughed and said, "Ancient, Thomas. Ancient."

Sarah cast Julia a withering look and said, "Oh, hush up, Child. Don't start with me. I still have a few tricks up my sleeve you know."

"Oh-oh. You'd better get ready for dinner Thomas before I get myself into more hot water." Julia laughed and ruffled the boy's hair.

"Okay, Julia. May I take my book with me?"

Sarah answered for her, "Of course, Thomas. It's yours now. A gift from your father."

As Thomas left the room with the book clutched in his small hands, Sarah said, "He's a delightful young man, Julia. You, Taryn, and Johann must all be quite proud of him."

"We are, Sarah. In addition to his endearing personality, he has a considerable amount of talent."

"So you have said. I'm looking forward to working with him and helping to shape his skills."

"I'm sure that he'll love working with you as much as Tay and I did." She paused and then said, "I'm sorry to be abrupt Sarah, but I'm anxious to see the sword before I speak with my brother this evening."

"Don't apologize, Julia. It's in your room under the bed. Be careful. It speaks of a powerful enchantment."

"I thought as much. It may take a great deal of work to remove the spell."

"Well if anyone can do it, you can. I'm sure that's why Taryn sent it to you."

"I'll go and study it now."

"What about your dinner? You need to eat."

"Don't worry about that, Sarah. This may take a while. I'll eat when I'm finished. Please tell Taryn what I'm doing if I'm a few moments late." With those words, Julia sprinkled some powder into the hearth. It was this powder that would direct the link to the appropriate hearth, thus keeping the siblings in touch no matter where their travels took them. As long as one of them used it, and the other was near a fire and open to receiving, the link would be established. Julia had developed and honed the powder over the intervening years since the fortuitous discovery when she and Taryn had been children.

Ever since their realization that Fire was an ally, the siblings had learned more and more ways in which to work with the flames. In addition to communication, they had discovered that they could send items back and forth through the hearth. That was how Thomas received his nightly gifts from his dad. The problem when sending items that way was that the flames burned off a bit of the item's energy and released it into the atmosphere. Normally this was not an issue as the energy dissipated quickly; however, the sword was powerful and Taryn was worried that the enemy camp's sorcerer might sense the brief energy burst and discover the cloaking spell he had put over the false sword. Thus, he had chosen the long and tedious, but safer, route of having the sword delivered by one of his most competent and trustworthy officers.

Julia went into the small bedroom which was hers when she stayed with Sarah. As she bent down to eye the object that was wrapped in leather and stored under the bed, she became aware of the energy emanating from the sword. Julia knew that this sword must hold a great deal of power if her brother had chosen to avoid their normal method of delivery.

As Julia eyed the wrapped sword, she took the time to call in protection for herself and everyone in the small cottage. Slowly, she withdrew the sword from underneath the bed and placed it on the mattress. She unwrapped the leather covering and saw the most magnificent weapon she had ever beheld. It was engraved with a dragon and set with a ruby at the hilt. As she scanned the energy with her hands, she could feel it pulsing almost as if it were alive.

When Julia was satisfied with her initial perusal, she covered the sword and returned it to its hiding place beneath the bed. Then she sat on the rocking chair in the small room, closed her eyes and began the slow, rhythmic breathing that helped her shift her consciousness to a deeper level. When she was ready, she used her thoughts to call in the protection of her animal allies and ancestors. As soon she sensed their arrival, she thanked them for their support and set her journey intention to meet her teacher Brigid.

In addition to animal allies, most enchanters also worked with a teacher. Many of these teachers were no longer alive, if they had ever lived at all, but still worked with select students who could journey to interact with them on other planes. Julia was fortunate to work with Brigid who was widely known as the goddess of hearth and was, among her many other talents, a skilled potion maker.

Julia envisioned herself leaving her body and walking into a heavy mist. Soon after, she exited the mist and arrived in a clearing in the forest where she and Brigid often met. There was a fire burning brightly and something simmering in a pot which hung over it. Brigid was standing by the fire with a long wooden spoon she used to stir the contents of the pot.

Welcome, Julia. This is a mighty undertaking we have before us.

I know, Brigid. This sword must have been embedded with power by a highly skilled sorcerer.

Indeed, it was. I recognize the work of a sorcerer named Razgar who has often been an aggravation to me over the years. Brigid looked meaningfully at her student. **I will enjoy returning the favor.**

What do we need to do? Taryn has masked the absence of the sword, but I don't think his spell will last for too long. We must proceed quickly, so that the sword can be returned to its owner before the cloak weakens.

First we must remove the power from the sword. Then we will place a spell on it so that the power appears to be the same to any who are sensitive to it. And lastly, we must cloak our work so that it cannot be traced backed to any of us. Razgar would only be too happy to demand retribution. Although I believe that we would win in the end, it would be a nasty battle and is best avoided.

Yes, please. We have enough battles at hand for now. What shall I do first?

I'm working on the removal potion; you can begin work on the spell to make it seem as if the sword is still

enchanted. Then together, we'll cloak our presence and Taryn's.

What about Sarah and the man who delivered the sword?

Of course. Good thinking. We'll put a memory spell on the sword so that it reads as if it never left the camp.

Perfect.

Meet me back here tomorrow. Before you come, you'll need to gather some herbs which you will use in your spellwork. They're most potent when harvested by moonlight.

Get your rest this evening. It's been a busy day, and you'll need all of your energy tomorrow in order to deal with this. This is quite a challenge that's been laid before us. I'll help you to prepare, but you must do the work yourself. You're ready for it. When you speak to Taryn, be sure to tell him of our plans.

I will, Brigid. Thank you.

Chapter Nineteen

Julia felt her higher self return to her waiting body which was seated in the room in Sarah's small cottage. She opened her eyes and allowed a moment to ground her energy. She had much work to do, but first, it was time for Taryn to check in; she wanted to speak with him before she went out to fetch the herbs she would need. As she opened the door to the living room, she heard Thomas giggling as he told his father about meeting the fairies.

"Ah, Thomas, I see that your aunt has finally arrived. Women often keep men waiting. It's a fact of life, Son. You might as well learn to live with it."

Julia shot her brother a look and said, "Hah. I was just giving you a taste of your own medicine."

"Okay. Off to bed, Son. Study hard and be good to Sarah and Nanny."

Thomas piped up. "What about Aunt Julia?"

Taryn responded with a shrug and a smile. "Don't worry about her. Your aunt can take care of herself."

"Okay. Night, Dad."

"Oh, and Thomas," he waited for his son to turn back to him, "no more straying off on your own."

"I know, Dad." He looked sincerely sorry, so Taryn knew the point had been made.

"I love you. See you tomorrow."

"I love you, too."

Julia smiled as she watched Thomas say his goodnights and leave the room followed by Nanny and Sarah. As soon as the siblings were alone, they quickly got down to business.

Taryn began. "Have you seen the sword yet?"

"Yes. It's a magnificent piece of work. It almost seems a shame to tamper with it."

"I know. I wish I had one myself."

Julia teased her brother. "Are you complaining about all of the protective work that I've done for you?" She placed her hands on her hips. "Because if you think that you can do better, go ahead and try."

"No, I'm not complaining." Taryn paused for emphasis. "Although sending a 6'4" protector is a bit much, don't you think, Julia?"

"Ah, so you've discovered Gern. My secret weapon. His one job is to keep your hide safe."

"You're lucky I like the big lug. He's a good sort." Taryn shrugged casually. "And if it puts your mind at ease, he can stay around. Besides he's a damn fine hunter. Many a meal has been consigned by his arrow."

"Good. Now back to the business at hand. Brigid and I will remove the power, put on a false power and protect our identities tomorrow morning. The sword will be ready to return by early evening at the latest."

"I'll send for it at sunset."

"Fine. You will need a way to get it back into the camp without detection. What have you decided upon?"

Taryn bristled a bit at his sister's peremptory tone. "Leave that to me, Julia. I got it out, didn't I? You know that I'm a master at this kind of thing."

Julia, realizing that she had overstepped, lightened the moment. "True. I remember many problems that you caused and I got blamed for."

Taryn smiled at his sister. "Neat trick, huh?" He paused and then continued on. "Listen, Jules, I hope you're not blaming yourself for what happened this morning. It could just as easily have happened with me."

"I know, Tay, but it was so frightening. And all I could think of was your dream." She sighed. "I guess that's one mystery solved."

"Maybe."

"You sound hesitant. Don't you think the dream was a warning about today?"

"I don't know. It doesn't feel right."

"How so?"

"Well, for one thing, it's always me in the dream that Thomas is separated from."

"That could be a symbol. Even though you weren't physically present, you would still be separated if something happened to him." When he didn't respond, she added, "What else?"

"The separation feels malevolent in the dreams. Almost as if someone is behind it. Today wasn't like that. It was a normal childhood occurrence."

She frowned as she thought for a moment. "Maybe you're right. I'll keep a close watch on him."

"I know you will. But not too close. Remember that boys get into scrapes. It's all part of growing up."

"Girls do, too."

He chuckled. "How well I remember."

Julia returned the smile and said, "Okay, enough banter. I have some serious work ahead of me. I want to get my rest tonight. I'll check in with you tomorrow."

"Okay. Good Luck."

Julia began readying herself for the task at hand as soon as the firelink was severed. First, she dealt with the sword. In order to have a comfortable night's sleep, Julia took the sword and wrapped it in her cloak which had its own enchantment woven into it. As the cloak was being made, a powerful sorcerer and fellow student of Brigid's had placed an energy-blocking spell in the very fabric. Normally, this protected the wearer from any energy being directed at her by others, but it could also be used, as in this case, to contain energy and not allow it to leak out.

By containing the energy of the sword, Julia would assure herself that no others could sense its presence and that she would get a good night's sleep. If the sword's enchantment were as powerful as Julia thought, it could seriously interfere with her sleep and send all sorts of strange dreams at the very least. At the worst, it could break through Taryn's cloaking spell and call its owner to the cottage to reclaim it. That was something that Julia could not allow.

As she finished wrapping the sword and placing it in a small wooden chest that was in the room, she heard the cawing of the rook outside her window. She quickly went outside to meet her.

What news, Reggie?

I waited to see the coachmen settled at the inn just to be sure that the spell had taken. All is fine. They were well into their cups and bragging about their recent army exploits. It's amazing that a small potion can help someone to create memories from nothing.

True. I have Brigid to thank for that potion - for all of my potions really. Brigid's a powerful teacher and ally. So are you my friend. Thank you for watching to be absolutely sure that all was well. You've gone above and beyond, as usual.

You said that this was important so I thought it best to double check - just to be absolutely sure.

Again, thank you. I'm wondering if you're open to one more task this evening?

What is it?

Brigid has asked me to gather some herbs by moonlight, and I could use your sharp eyes to help me spot them in the forest.

Fine. Will the Wolf accompany us?

I think that would be wise, as I don't know these woods quite as well as the ones near the castle. It's been years since I played in them with Tay. I'll call for the Wolf.

When the Wolf appeared, the companions set off in search of the herbs. Some of them were herbs that she had never worked with and might not have recognized, but Brigid had placed a spell around them and given them a glow which drew the eyes of the three searchers. After their task was complete, the trio returned to the clearing by the small cottage, and the allies took their leave. Then, Julia took a final moment to tap in and check that all was well back at the castle. When she was satisfied that everyone was safe for the time being, she composed a note which she would have Reggie deliver in the morning and which told her father that she had gone away with Thomas and Nanny and would return within a fortnight. She felt guilty that her father had to learn of the trio's journey this way, but she had seen no other options that were as safe.

Chapter Twenty

The next morning was a bit overcast, but Thomas was bright-eyed and ready to learn by the time Julia emerged from her room. Sarah was just preparing to send him off to look for a root which was found by the edge of the pond.

"Now take Nanny with you, and be careful that you don't slip and fall into the water. It's a bit chilly at this time of year."

"Okay, Sarah. How many roots should I find? "

"Don't return until you have at least five as we will need that many for the poultice."

"What's pull-tish?"

"Poultice. It's a paste that we make from different roots and apply for healing. In this case, we wrap it around sprained or broken limbs. It helps to lock them in one place so that they can heal more effectively." She winked at him. "We might as well start with something practical."

"When can we work with the Fairyweed?"

"We'll do something with that this afternoon, Thomas. Now off with you."

"Bye, Sarah. Bye, Julia." He reached for Nanny's hand and gave it a tug. "Come on, Nanny. We have work to do!"

Julia laughed as she heard the words that she often said to Thomas echoed in the young boy's speech. After they had gone, she turned to Sarah and explained the spell work that she would be doing this morning. "I'm going to need to remain uninterrupted for a period of time Sarah."

"Why do you think I sent Thomas and Nanny out to the pond? It will take them a few hours to locate and dig up the roots that they are assigned to find."

"That's great. Thanks."

"I'm going outside myself to sit in the sun and await my young student's return. I also want to make sure that he and Nanny don't end up in the pond by mistake."

Julia laughed. "Good thinking. I'll be using the main living area as I'll need the hearth for much of my work." Sarah gathered up her knitting and some tea while Julia set about compiling all of the tools that she would need to remove the enchantment from the sword.

As Sarah settled in on the front lawn, Julia completed her preparation for the work which she would undertake this morning. She set the sword, still wrapped in the cloak, on the kitchen table along with her herbs and powders. Then she brought out her objects of power. These pieces consisted of presents from teachers she had worked with - crystals, rattles and the like, and presents from the magical folk. The fairies had gifted her with a garland of baby's breath which she placed on her head, and Brigid had led her to different stones and shells which held power and which she now placed at strategic points around the work area.

Julia knew that she could do the work without the physical objects. She had been taught not to rely on anything that could be taken from her or lost as a source of her power; however, she also knew that, when available to her, these pieces could ease the way and give her a helpful boost of energy. That was why she always carried a small pouch filled with her power objects. The process she was about to undertake would most likely be a tedious and difficult one, and she wanted to call upon every available ally for assistance.

After setting up her physical tools, Julia called in her spiritual power. She called to the four directions, Father Sun and Mother Earth, her ancestors, allies and teachers. She asked for protection while she worked and help in accomplishing her goal. As the call-in progressed, Julia could feel a shift in the atmosphere around her. She felt the air become heavier and hotter as her allies came to assist. She thanked them all for the gift of their teachings and protection, and sat down, ready to finally begin her journey to Brigid, secure in the knowledge that she was protected and aided.

She closed her eyes and slowed her breathing as she shifted into a journey state. In this light trance, Julia was vaguely aware of her surroundings in the cottage but not distracted by them. When she knew that she was ready, she set forth her intention of meeting up with her teacher. She felt her higher self step out of her body, walk through the mist, and arrive in the forest clearing where she met Brigid. Once again, she spotted her teacher by a large kettle which was simmering over the open fire.

Brigid turned to her and said, **Welcome, Julia. We have much to do today. I have readied a powerful spell which will remove the protection from the sword.**

The Sorcerer's protection spell was originally burned into the sword with the heat of a dragon's breath; thus the markings on the side of it. Therefore, we will need the heat from your fire to be even hotter and more powerful in order to burn off the original spell. I hope you gathered the herbs we'll need to intensify the flame in Sarah's hearth.

Yes. We gathered them last night. They're on the table at Sarah's.

Good.

With that said, Brigid proceeded to instruct Julia as to the appropriate steps to take to remove the spell. After Julia was sure that she understood, she thanked her mentor and journeyed back to begin the complex process of spell removal.

First Julia stoked the flame in the hearth with some firewood. When it was burning hot, she added the herbs and powders which were needed to bring the flame to an even higher temperature. She then moved to the sword and unwrapped the mighty weapon. She couldn't help but admire its beauty and craftsmanship and hoped that someday her brother Taryn would have as magnificent a weapon to wield.

Next, she placed the sword in the fire and recited the incantation that Brigid had taught her as well as some spell removal work that she had learned before. As soon as the saw the spell lift in a small puff of smoke, she threw the powders into the small cloud. Some of the powders would dispel the energy of the original enchantment while others placed a temporary cloaking spell on the sword. It was crucial that these two pieces occur simultaneously; there could be no time lapse between the destruction of one spell and the creation of the other. A time lapse would have been almost impossible to cover and would have alerted the enemy to the tampering which Julia was doing now.

When Julia was satisfied that the first portion of the task was complete, she performed the permanent cloaking of the sword's memory. In this way, the energy in the sword would reflect that it had always been in the army camp and had never been removed or worked on. It would also prevent a tracing of Julia and Taryn by the sorcerer for Royce's camp.

When Julia was satisfied with the work she had done on the sword, she sat in the rocker, placed the sword across her lap and journeyed back to the clearing to Brigid to confirm her belief that her work was complete.

Fine job, Julia. You are an apt student.

Have I done all that I need to do, Brigid?

Almost. Burn the cloth that your brother carried the sword in and wrap it in one of Sarah's that holds no special power. That will keep any old energy from coming off on the sword when Gern comes to collect it tonight.

Gern is coming?

Yes. Your brother thought that you might like to see him. Not to mention that he is goading you about sending Gern to watch over him.

Julia replied, *He can goad me all he damn well pleases as long as he lets Gern stay and watch his back.*

Brigid smiled at the sister's need to protect her younger brother. **Now, Julia, you know that he's just teasing you. If he really minded, he would have removed Gern from service.**

Julia had to concede that one. *That's true. I just want to keep him safe. Thank you again for all of your help doing that as well, Brigid.*

I want you both to be safe.

Julia waved her hand in dismissal. *There's no need to worry about me. It's Taryn who's risking his neck every day.*

Don't be too complacent about your own safety.

Julia stared at her teacher as the meaning of her words became clear. *What are you saying, Brigid? Am I in some danger?*

The future is not fully decided. You'll have choices to make which will determine your fate.

Isn't that always so?

Yes, but this time there are powerful forces at work against you. Don't take them lightly. They will test you in ways that you've never been tested before. Brigid paused, realizing that she had alarmed her young student. Her tone was gentle as she continued. I have faith in you and Taryn. You are each powerful in your own right; together you can do most anything.

Julia's forehead creased. *Brigid, please, tell me. Is there something I should be worried about?*

Julia, you know as well as I do that a teacher is not supposed to interfere with a student's destiny or free will. You must learn your own lessons.

Julia felt a chill run down her back as she listened to her teacher's none-too-subtle warning. *Perhaps with more details, I could prepare for whatever is coming.*

You cannot plan for that which isn't yet decided, Julia. But I can give you some advice if you will listen.

Always.

In the past, you've been told not to count on your physical tools as a source of power. They may be taken from you or used against you. Know that your human senses and intellect can be fooled as well. Remember your strength always lies within you. Trust what you know in your heart to be true. Your connection to all that you love is a deep core which will center and empower you. With that, Brigid leaned over and kissed Julia on the cheek.

Julia was overwhelmed by this turn of events. She needed and wanted more information, but reluctantly realized that she would get no more from her teacher; it would be futile to push. *Thank you, Brigid. I know that it must be hard for you to stand by and watch a student make her own mistakes. I am indeed blessed to have you in my life, and I'm grateful for your advice. I will remember all you have done to help me.*

Good-bye, Child. Be safe.

~~~~~~~~~~~~~~~

Julia opened her eyes to find herself seated in the rocking chair with the sword in her lap. She was gripping the sword hilt so hard that the dragon's head had imprinted into her palm. She spent a moment flexing her sore hand and trying to make sense of her teacher's warning. Reluctantly realizing that this was not the time for rumination, Julia got up and threw Taryn's original wrapping into the fire, rewrapped the sword in a plain piece of Sarah's cloth, and put it back under her bed. Then she set about packing up all of her magical objects, powders, and herbs.

Just as she finished cleaning up and making sure that there was no trace of the cloth remaining in the fire, the door opened and Thomas ran into the room. He was followed by Nanny and Sarah who said, "Reggie told Thomas it was safe to return. Is all well in here?"

"Everything's fine, Sarah. I used a piece of your plain cloth to wrap the item in. I hope that's all right."

"Of course, Julia. You don't need to ask. Now how about if I fix some lunch while Thomas tells you of his morning's pursuits. He has had quite a successful beginning to his work as an herbal healer."

Julia beckoned to Thomas who sat on her lap and chatted happily about his adventures finding the roots. As she listened with one ear, Julia thought ahead to what the next few days would hold for her. It was imperative that she check in with her allies and that she try to decipher the specifics behind Brigid's vague warning. In addition, she looked forward to seeing Gern again and hearing news of the war from his mouth.

She knew that Taryn was usually honest with her, but he might make light of anything that he thought would cause her undue worry. The siblings rarely lied to each other, but they were not above an occasional omission of part of their story. That was one of the reasons Julia wanted Gern's opinion. She was beginning to suspect that the man had developed a crush on her, but she also knew that he would give her the unembellished truth regarding her brother and the war with Royce. That information made suffering through a few starry-eyed looks worth it for Julia.

Chapter Twenty-One

The unembellished truth was exactly what Taryn was planning on sharing with his father. It was time that he update the man on the progress, or lack thereof, of this war. For the life of him, Taryn couldn't understand how his father expected to protect the territory by simply holding the border. They needed to go on the offense.

Taryn looked forward to sharing the story of the sword with his father. Perhaps that would make Johann realize that there would be bloodshed before this siege would end. There was no reason that Royce commissioned that sword unless he planned on Carlson's using it. And that surely meant the death of more of Johann's soldiers.

In addition to breaking that news to his father, Taryn also knew that he would take the brunt of Johann's anger for the way that Julia, with his permission, had spirited Thomas away from the castle. Johann would be angry and worried, and Taryn would have to let him vent for a while before he got a word in edgewise.

Taryn had decided to have Gern accompany him to the castle and then ride on to pick up the sword afterwards. The castle was halfway to Sarah's and only a little out of the way, so it made sense for the men to ride together. That should also cheer Gern up as he would be "keeping an eye" on Taryn as per Julia's orders.

He went to find his bodyguard who was doing some arms coaching in a nearby field. When Gern spotted him, he hurried over to Taryn's side.

"What's happening, boss?"

"Gern, I'm riding to the castle this morning. I need to update my father on the situation here. I wonder if you might like to accompany me and then ride off to fetch the sword afterwards. Julia said that it would be ready by nightfall, and I thought you might be the one to pick it up. It would, after all, give you a chance to report on me to your real boss."

Taryn watched as the large man blushed and looked at the ground. "Good grief, Gern. I already told you that I know about your being hired by Julia." Taryn paused, studied the man, and then added teasingly, "The way you're acting, I'd almost say that you had something else you were hiding from me. Perhaps another secret involving Julia." Taryn watched as Gern's blush turned an even deeper shade of red. Then it occurred to him just what the secret was. "Well, I'll be damned," he chuckled. "You big lug. You've gone and fallen for Julia, haven't you?"

Gern tried to deny it to Taryn, just as he had tried to deny it to himself. "No, sir. That would be terribly inappropriate... I just...uh..." He sighed as he realized how futile his protests were.

Taryn clapped him on the shoulder and laughed. "That settles it then. You'll ride with me to the castle and then off you are to see your one true love."

As Gern turned to make his way to the horses he said, "Aye, and I'll never be hearing the end of this one, will I?"

Taryn laughed out loud. "Are you kidding? This is far too good to let go. I'm going to enjoy myself heartily as compensation for all of the times you've stuck to me like a burr in my side." Taryn shook his head in mock despair. "Here I thought that you cared about me, now I know it's been Julia all along." Then he added in a dreamy, lovesick voice, "Julia, Julia, Julia," and followed that with a sigh.

Gern reached out and cuffed him on the shoulder. "You'd best be remembering who watches your backside."

"Ha! It's not **my** backside you've been watching."

Gern shook his head and swatted his big hand through the air as if to dislodge an annoying fly. Then he turned away and went to saddle the horses while Taryn informed their fellow officers of the plans. Gern could hear his boss whistling the wedding march as he left and knew that he was destined for a ride full of teasing at his expense. He only hoped that Taryn wouldn't embarrass him in front of Julia the next time that they were all together. He'd rather die than have her know about the feelings he had for her - feelings that he was sure she would never reciprocate.

Chapter Twenty-Two

The pleasant journey to the castle went all too quickly and Taryn was left to confront his father while Gern fed and groomed the horses and gathered up some supplies for the army. Before they parted, the two men arranged a meeting time to update each other on the day's errands and for Taryn to collect the supplies. After that, Gern would journey on ahead to Sarah's, and Taryn would ride back to the camp.

Taryn found Johann pacing alone in his meeting room. "Taryn! It's about time you showed your face. Your sister has really done it this time."

"I know all about it, Father."

"What? You were part of this? How could you let her take Thomas off the land during this attack?"

"Father, calm down. We didn't tell you because we didn't want to worry you."

"Well, that's exactly what you have done. How could you two be so damn inconsiderate?"

"The place they are staying is not only farther from the fighting, but a far less likely target."

"That's all fine and well, but who is guarding Thomas?"

"Julia is, and you know as well as I do that she will protect her nephew with her life."

"And that's supposed to make me feel better?"

Taryn smiled. "I wouldn't want to be the army that faces Julia. Would you?"

Johann reluctantly conceded that point, and after a few more minutes of conversation and reassurances, he had calmed down enough that Taryn was able to redirect the conversation to other recent occurrences. As Taryn told his father about the poison that had been used on him and the sword and its mystical powers, he became more and more frustrated. No matter how hard he tried to convince his father of the necessity of an offensive attack, his father was equally adamant about not escalating the conflict. Finally Taryn's emotions boiled over.

"Father, we have to move on this. This man will decimate us if we allow him to. All because of this ridiculous decision you have made not to fight. Sometimes you have to fight to protect what is yours. I will not stand by and watch men that I care about be slaughtered or the land be taken because **you** are afraid."

Taryn's tone was condescending and Johann responded to it. He turned on his son and erupted. "What do you know of being a coward or a brave man? You are too impulsive, Son, and too sure of your own powers. That will be your undoing if you're not careful. I know. It was my own arrogance and desire for power that cost my wife and child their lives. And I won't have it happen again. Not while I'm alive." Silence hung heavily in the air as Johann regretted his hastily spoken words.

Taryn stared. He was reeling from his father's rare outburst. "Father, how can you say such a thing? It's well known that Mother and the baby died in childbirth."

"Yes, Son. You're correct in what you know, but you don't know the whole story." Suddenly the fire went out of Johann's eyes and with it the temper that had overtaken him. He sighed and sat down. "Perhaps it is time that I shared your full legacy with you. Then you will understand the consequences of underestimating your enemy or fighting too rashly. Sit down." He motioned to the chair beside his, and Taryn moved to join him.

All of the ire, which had been present in Johann only a moment earlier, had been replaced by a sorrow which ran much deeper. "Taryn, as you know, you had a younger brother. He and your mother died in childbirth while I was away fighting a different war. What you may not know is that it is my fault that they died."

Taryn shook his head in denial. "How can you say that?"

Johann raised his hand to stop his son from further interrupting. "Let me tell you the tale. It's time that you heard the full story and that you understand why, this time, I am trying to make decisions with my head and my heart and not my foolish pride."

Taryn waited expectantly as Johann took a deep breath and began. "As you know, our right to rule has been challenged before. A long time ago, Lord Jeffers was looking to expand his territory and take over our land as well as the land to our northwest. His advance was meeting with much success, not because his army was better than all the others or his cause more worthy, but because he had a powerful wizard at his side. This wizard's name was Razgar, and he was behind Jeffers' rapid ascent to power and ultimate destruction," he paused, "but I am getting ahead of myself."

"Razgar came to work with Jeffers - at what price I do not know, but I can only assume that it was a high price. I know that it was too high for me to pay. You see, Razgar had first offered his services to me. At the time, you had just been born and my healer had died of old age. Razgar showed up at the castle and convinced your mother that he would be the perfect man to teach you and Julia, work by my side, and care for the sick in our village. It seemed too good to be true, and indeed it was."

"Once your dear mother left the room, Razgar informed me of the price that I would pay for these services. He had a young son, about ten or so, who had been training with the Druids in the Highlands, and I was to adopt his son and make him my own child. He was to have all of the privileges of a full heir and even more for, as the eldest child, he would take over the kingdom upon my death. In exchange, Razgar promised all of us long lives, no wars, rich crops, and healthy and happy people in our villages. To seal the deal, he stated that you and Julia would be allowed to live in the castle as siblings to his son, but you would have no ruling power and only minor land titles."

"This was outrageous, so of course I turned him down and banished him from my lands immediately. He was enraged and issued threat after threat, even as he was escorted out by the guard. Foolishly, I ignored his ranting and quickly forgot about him."

"Shortly thereafter, I learned that Jeffers had struck a deal with Razgar, and the man was now in place as his wizard. Not surprisingly, Jeffers' Highland territory began to flourish. The more he had, the more he wanted, and it was only a few years later that Jeffers started to expand his land by taking over

94

the weaker settlements. Soon he began to look in our direction, and I knew that we would have to fight. By this time, you and Julia were young children."

"Also around this time, your mother became pregnant with your younger brother. It was not an easy pregnancy which struck us as odd since the first two had been pleasant and simple. Your mother's pregnancy served to remind me that we needed a healer, but unfortunately, I had to turn my attention to the war which Jeffers and Razgar were raging against our land. They proved to be powerful enemies, and it was clear that we would have to march out to meet and fight them. So I formed an army. I hated to leave your mother who was in her third month, but we agreed that it was necessary, and so my men and I journeyed north and prepared to wage war and stop Jeffers' advance. Luckily, Lord Emil to our northwest agreed to join armies and to fight as one as his territory was in danger from Jeffers as well. This is probably the only thing that saved us... that and the death of Razgar's son."

By now, Taryn was leaning forward in his seat. He had never before heard the tale that his father was spinning, but he was certain of its impact on his father's life. He had a strong feeling that the reason for many of his father's seemingly incongruous decisions would soon become a lot clearer.

"Weeks and then months passed, and the war was going poorly for us. Every time we advanced and won a battle, the tides would turn and we would lose the next few. Our men were despondent and exhausted. I was constantly worried about your mother and you children and wondering how the pregnancy had progressed. The news I received was sporadic at best, and most of it confirmed that your mother was not doing well although she was putting up a brave front at home. But even with all of that, I would not give up and return home. No one was going to challenge my right to rule. Fighting and besting the enemy became the only objective I could focus on. I was blind to what really mattered."

"Emil and I decided that the time had come to make one last stand and to fight until the end. We would either win or die fighting. We planned a stealth attack on Jeffers' camp in the middle of the night. We knew enough to be careful not to project our thoughts for Razgar to pick up on. Indeed, we didn't even share our plans with the men until the night of the attack."

"We raided the enemy camp and killed many of Jeffer's men while they slept. Not the most honorable way to do battle, but one that we justified under the circumstances."

"In the chaos that ensued, many innocent camp followers were also slaughtered including Razgar's son. I take full responsibility for his death even though it wasn't my sword that performed the deed. I was in command; I am to be blamed." In a weary gesture, Johann held his head in his hands.

"The carnage was staggering. There were dead bodies all over the field - ours and mostly theirs. And the women and children..." At this moment, Johann paused in the telling of the story. In his mind, he was reliving the sight of that field littered with the dead. His visage looked far older than his years as he wearily shook his head. "As long as I live, I will never forget that sight." Johann sighed, squared his shoulders and said, "Obviously, after this rout, Jeffers was forced to retreat and, shortly later, admit defeat."

"We packed up camp and started the journey home. The mood was a strange combination of victorious and somber. Too much blood had been shed and too many innocent lives were lost for us to claim a guilt-free victory, and yet those of us left were relieved to have survived."

"En route home, we stopped at Emil's castle and gave the men a chance to relax and enjoy themselves. We felt that they deserved it after their unstinting devotion to us and our cause. If only I had pushed the men and hurried home, I might have even then saved your mother and the baby. That is one of the many sorrows that I will carry to my grave." Johann paused for a moment and gathered strength to finish the tale that he had begun. Although he had often replayed these moments privately, this was the first he had spoken of them to anyone, and he found himself haunted by the memories and ghosts of the dead.

"While the army was at Emil's, your mother went into labor and struggled to give birth. It was almost as if something, or someone, had cursed her. Nothing went smoothly. As I hadn't had time to find a healer before I left to fight, poor Nanny Magret was doing the best she could to care for you, Julia, and your mother. It appeared to be a stroke of luck that a traveling minister passed though and offered to help Margret with your mother's care."

"The minister stayed with Nanny while your mother was in labor. The baby wasn't coming easily, but after a long labor your mother finally gave birth to your brother. She was so weakened by the ordeal that she became feverish and delusional. Nanny said that she held onto the minister and begged forgiveness for her past deeds. Evidently her ramblings weren't coherent and to ease her agitated mind, the minister gave her some medicine. After that, your mother finally relaxed and fell asleep. It was agreed that while your mother slept, Nanny would rest as well. The minister sent her off to her room with assurances that he would remain with your mother and alert Nanny if she were needed."

"Several hours later, Nanny awoke and went to see your mother and brother. When she entered the room, she was confronted by a horrible sight. Your mother had hemorrhaged. There was blood everywhere, she was dead, and your baby brother had suffocated under her body. We could only surmise that she must have unknowingly rolled over on him in her feverish state. The minister was never heard from or seen again. The only thing of his that was left behind was a crystal."

"A crystal? What kind of crystal?"

"I don't know, Son. By the time that I arrived home, Nanny had removed the crystal, and not knowing when I would return, she had your mother and brother buried. She thought it best not to further traumatize you and your sister, so she arranged for a simple ceremony and burial. My grief was so overwhelming and my guilt so intense that I didn't think to ask questions for months. Poor Nanny was a wreck too. We actually brought her friend Sarah to the castle to help care for you and Julia while Nanny got back on her feet. I'm sure that it's only because of the two of you that either of us survived that terrible ordeal. We had to go on for you."

Taryn, thinking back to the death of his beloved Celia, understood his father's grief all too well. "I can understand that.

I know that Thomas forced me to continue living when I would have preferred to join Celia in the grave."

His father nodded slowly. "Then perhaps you can understand why it took me months to see that there were many unanswered questions about your mother's death. Who was the traveling minister who just happened by? What was in the medicine that your mother was given to drink? Why was a crystal left behind?"

"I never received adequate answers to those questions - perhaps because there were none. I suspected foul play on Razgar's part, but I never had any proof. He might have decided that he would take your mother and brother's lives in revenge for the death of his son, but I can't be sure of that. I never heard from him again."

"Word from travelers that passed through was that he deserted Jeffers and went into seclusion in the Highlands. I decided to let him be as I didn't have the heart to fight any longer, and I didn't want anything to happen to you or your sister. Both Razgar and I had suffered our tragedies. It seemed wiser to end the fighting before there was more loss on either side."

After a pause, he continued. "For some time, I have suspected that Razgar might be behind the renewed attack on our people. The enchantment of the sword seems to support that theory. I must tell you, Taryn, that he is a powerful sorcerer, and I am none too fond of our fighting him again. We barely survived the first round."

Taryn looked directly into his father's eyes. He knew that he owed the man a great deal, not the least of which was honesty. "We have no other option, Father. We have to make a stand."

"I know, Son. That's apparent now." Johann sighed. "I need some time to think. Let's meet again tomorrow and discuss our plans."

Taryn looked at his father and saw the years of worry and stress. Suddenly, he realized the burden that his father had carried alone through all of those years. He stood and put his arm around his father's shoulders. "Dad, you did the best that you could do; this wasn't your fault."

Johann sighed. The catharsis that should have come with the telling of the tale was nowhere to be found. Instead he felt as if an enormous mantle of sorrow and regret were resting upon his shoulders. "That's not how it feels. Every day the weight of all those deaths is on me. So many lost because I was too quick to fight and too proud to offer a compromise. So many families who lost loved ones because of orders I gave." He rested his head in his hands. "Now if you don't mind..."

"Of course." Taryn took his leave and went outside to breathe some fresh air. He was chagrined that he had been so quick to judge. He should have known that there would be a reason behind the decision. Now he would wait and respect the time that his father needed. That meant that he would be away from camp for one more night while his father made some decisions. That short amount of time was the least that Johann deserved.

Taryn would send Skye to his officers with word of his delay. As he wrote the note which Skye would deliver, Taryn felt the weight of his legacy settle fully on his shoulders. He needed time to digest the story which his father had shared, but he couldn't help but want to step away from it for a while.

Suddenly, he knew exactly how he would spend the night. He needed to see someone who could remind him of what he loved most in this world. He would ride out as soon as he found Gern.

But first, there was certain young lady that he wanted to visit.

Chapter Twenty-Three

Back at Sarah's cottage, the rest of the day passed in a peaceful manner. Julia joined Thomas for a while as he learned about the Fairyweed. Over night, he had decided that he would build the fairies a home out of twigs and moss and that he and Julia would hang it in a tree near the fairy bower on the journey home. In it, he would place special items that he found or created to make their home more comfortable.

After his afternoon lessons, Julia and Thomas went for a walk in the forest so that he could look for twigs and other natural materials suitable to build the home, and Julia could check in with the Wolf and her pack.

The Wolf joined them as soon as they entered the forest. After they spent some time gathering supplies, the Wolf led them to the rest of her pack who had been awaiting their arrival. While Thomas and Julia watched with delight, the older wolves set about training the young ones. The cubs were so cute that Julia had all she could do to keep Thomas from wanting to play with them, but it was important that the cubs learn their lessons just as Thomas was learning his. This left Julia and Thomas relegated to the sidelines to watch the mock battles that the older cubs engaged in with the younger and the brief hunting forays that took place.

While they were seated and enjoying the wolf engagements, Thomas turned to his aunt and asked a question that he had been pondering for a few days now.

"Aunt Julia?"

"Yes, Thomas."

"The Tiger is my ally just like the Wolf is yours. Right?"

"Right." She flinched as one of the young cubs was pounced upon by an unseen 'stalker.'

Thomas was silent for a moment. "Then why can everyone see your ally and only some people can see mine?"

Julia, who had been distracted while watching the wolves, now turned her full attention to her nephew. He had asked a complex question. Julia wanted to honor his need to know without overwhelming him with information that was too advanced for him to handle at five years old.

"The world we live in has different realities Thomas, but not everyone is aware of those realities."

He looked at his aunt and frowned as he tried to understand what she was saying.

Julia continued, "People live in one reality. It is the world which we can all see." She waved her hand over the scene before them. "There are also worlds, or realities, that most people can't see. Many of these realities overlap with ours in different magical places, and some people, like us, can see them.

"Like where the fairies live?"

"Exactly!" Julia felt a sense of relief that he was understanding her. "Most people would walk right past the fairies and never see them."

"But why can everyone see the Wolf?"

"Because the Wolf lives in two realities, the one we inhabit, and the one that is magical."

"The Tiger only lives in the magical one?"

"Right."

Thomas frowned in concentration. "What if I want him to live here?"

Julia laughed and threw her arm over his shoulder. "That would make a lot of people very nervous. Can you imagine explaining to Nanny why there is a Tiger in your room?"

Thomas giggled. "Maybe that's why Tiger stays in the other reality. Nanny can be very scary!"

"Yes, she can." She smiled at her nephew. "Of course, Tigers are pretty scary too."

"But how can Tiger scare anyone if they can't see him?"

She contemplated how to best answer his question. "Think about this, Thomas. What scares you more? Something you can see or something that you know is there but you can't see."

He opened his eyes wide with recognition. "So Tiger **can** protect me!"

"Absolutely. You, my favorite child, are protected so well and by so many that no one will ever harm you." She pulled him closer and kissed him on the head. Feeling once more how fierce her love for him was, she held him to her side for a moment. When he began to squirm, she realized that she might unintentionally frighten him with the intensity of her emotions. She loosened her grip on him and shifted so that she could look into his eyes. "Some day, when you learn to journey, you can visit those magical realities whenever you want to, just as your father and I do."

"I think I'll like that, Julia." He looked at her and smiled.

"I think you will, too. It's a precious gift that we are honored to accept."

Satisfied that Thomas had his questions answered for now, Julia stood, held her hand out to him, and the two started the short journey back to Sarah's cottage just as the sun was setting. As Julia scanned the orange and red horizon, the Rook flew in and landed on a nearby tree.

Two riders approach.

Who are they?

They are friendly. They wear the blue and green. Here to gather the sword.

Why two? I knew of Gern's arrival, but who is accompanying him?

The Rook hesitated and shifted her weight. **A fellow soldier.**

Hmm. That seems a waste of manpower - not like my brother at all.

Perhaps the second rider has a different mission from the first.

Perhaps. Either way, we'd best hurry to the cottage to meet them. Thank you, Reggie.

Julia turned to Thomas who had wandered a short distance to finish collecting twigs and gifts for the Fairy house. "C'mon TomCat. It's time for us to go back to Sarah's. Gern is coming to collect the sword I was working on."

"Just one second, Aunt Julia. I'm almost done. Can you hold these for me?" Feeling sure of the answer, Thomas proceeded to give Julia another bunch of twigs for the bag that she had slung over her shoulder. After about twenty more minutes of gathering, Julia's bag was overflowing.

"Thomas, you have enough for five fairy houses!"

"But only one castle, Julia. I'm going to build them a castle!"

Julia raised an eyebrow and looked at the small child whose own eyes shone brightly with his enthusiasm. "I'm sure that they will be delighted with whatever you choose to make for them. Okay, finish up. The sun is setting. Soon it will be difficult to see the path back."

"I'm sure the Wolf will lead us if you ask her to. Dad says they can see really well in the dark."

"Dad's right, but it really is time to go and help Sarah fix dinner."

Suddenly, Julia heard a twig snap slightly off the path and ahead of them. She tried briefly to tap in and learn more, but whatever was out there was stealthy. It had, however, given itself away with the snap of a twig. She glanced at the Wolf whose head was cocked but whose hackles were not raised and knew immediately who was stalking them. She motioned to Thomas to join her quietly. He looked at her with big, frightened eyes, and she leaned in.

"Thomas, Gern is trying to sneak up on us. Let's play a little game and prove to him that he can't catch us too easily. Want to do that?"

Thomas nodded his head and stared at Julia for a cue as to their next step. Julia turned to the Wolf and thought, *Want to play with us?*

Of course.

Good. You hide behind the knoll and growl as he approaches. Just be careful not to get shot.

Don't worry, Julia. I know this stalker as well as he knows me.

Julia signaled to Thomas to follow her as quietly as possible. As they crept along, she reflected on the fact that this was the human version of the wolf cub training that they had watched all afternoon. These games would help to make Thomas sharp for the day when someone was stalking him with malice in mind.

She was sure that this was why the twig had snapped. Gern was providing her with a chance to give Thomas a little

103

training. She'd have to remember to congratulate him on his good thinking. On second thought, with the crush the big lug had on her, she might just keep her kindness to herself. Really, he made it humiliatingly obvious. She only hoped that her brother would never discover it. Taryn would have far too much fun seeing Gern become all tongue-tied and school-boyish around his sister.

Julia's thoughts were interrupted by another twig snapping - this one much closer than the last. She heard the Wolf growl her warning and motioned to Thomas to get ready to attack. Thomas' excitement was so intense that Julia wondered if he'd be able to hold still long enough for the signal. Suddenly she felt the air shift and knew that the time was right. She motioned to Thomas, and they flew out from behind the tree to confront... her brother!

"Daddy!" Thomas launched himself into his father's arms and the two rolled onto the forest floor.

"Argh. You got me. I never would have known you were there."

The two laughed and tumbled around, all the while being careful of Thomas' arm. When they were finished, Taryn greeted his sister with a somewhat more subdued, but equally loving, greeting.

"Hello, Sis. I thought you might miss me. Besides I couldn't stand not seeing you and Gern together."

"Ha-ha. Very funny, Tay." Julia grimaced and made a face at her brother. Obviously he had discerned Gern's growing interest. "It is good to see your ugly hide though." She leaned over Thomas and gave him a hug.

"Yeah, I thought I could take a break for a short while."

Julia's sharp eyes noticed the weariness that flashed over his face. "What's happening?"

Taryn looked at her meaningfully while pointedly keeping his tone light. "Not much. We can talk later."

Taking her cue, Julia nodded and changed the subject. "You'll stay the night then?"

"We leave at first light. That's all the time away that we can afford, Jules."

"Well, we're happy to see you even if only for a short while."

That was the last word Julia was to get in edgewise for quite a while as Thomas quickly began chatting about all of the exciting happenings in his life. As the trio cleared the forest and headed toward the cottage, the door opened and Gern came stumbling out. Good Grief. Had the man been watching for them? She turned to see her brother wink at her and hear him whisper, "Be nice."

"Be nice," she mimicked. Men!

Julia stoically tolerated the effusively bumbling greeting from Gern and the small group went into the cottage to help Sarah with dinner. Gern quickly calmed down and the next several hours were filled with stories and conversation as everyone shared his or her news. After Thomas made a reluctant trip to bed and Nanny and Sarah were settled in as well, the group finally got down to discussing serious business.

Julia shared the process she had undertaken to remove the spell and energetic memory from the sword while Taryn and Gern shared the plan to get it back into camp.

"Are you sure that it's safe, Tay?"

"As safe as possible. Skye and Gern both have my back, and I couldn't think of two allies that I'd want there more." Gern blushed at the praise. "Except for you, of course, Sis."

"Of course," Julia said with a sarcastic tone.

"Now Jules, don't be like that."

"Like what? You get to be part of the action while I'm stuck holding down the home front."

Taryn sighed as they headed down the same old road. They had had this conversation several times in the past. "Julia, we've discussed this over and over. One of us has to stay at home to protect the family, and one of us has to lead the army. No offense, but I don't think the men would be any too happy to have a female as their leader."

"I know, I know." As always, Julia had to concede that point to him.

In order to make her feel somewhat more involved, Taryn and Gern then explained their military plans to her and solicited her advice on troop movement should Johann agree to let them go on the offensive. Taryn had to admit that she had a good head on her shoulders for strategy, and he listened to her opinions with an open mind.

After Gern retired for the evening, Taryn filled Julia in on the family story that their father had shared. When Julia heard Razgar's name mentioned, she shared Brigid's warning about the sorcerer with her brother and promised to journey back to get more information from her teacher tomorrow.

Finally the time came, and Taryn knew he had to be completely honest. "There's one more thing before we go to bed."

"What is it, Tay?"

"Do you remember that wound on my shoulder?"

"Of course."

"There's something I didn't tell you about it."

"Go on." Julia's voice was level as she kept her irritation in check. She knew that Taryn would shut down if she got angry with him now.

Taryn winced as he correctly guessed her reaction to his next statement. "It seems the sword had been treated with poison."

"Tay!"

"Now stay calm, Julia. I already did some work on an antidote."

"Tell me everything, and **don't** leave anything out."

After Taryn finished his tale, Julia set to work. She took the bottle of poison which Skye had obtained and did her own analysis. Taryn kept her company offering suggestions and lending a hand when needed. At one point, he sheepishly noted that Julia had uncovered an ingredient in the poison which he had overlooked. That minor mistake could be the reason that he was still afflicted with the dizziness. Only time would tell.

After he had taken the new antidote, Julia said, "That should do the trick, but if you have any more dizzy spells, let me know…immediately."

Taryn saluted her and grinned, "Aye, aye, Captain."

Julia glared at him and put her hands firmly on her hips. "I'm not kidding, Tay. This is nothing to joke about." Tears began to well up in her eyes.

Taryn saw them and grabbed her in a bear hug. "I'll be fine, Jules. Don't go all mushy on me."

She swatted his arm. "You'd better be!"

All too soon it was time for the siblings to say good night to one another. Before they parted, Julia extracted several promises from Taryn to contact her immediately if the antidote wasn't working completely. Since the poison had been in his bloodstream for a few days, it may take a while to completely eradicate it. She sent him off with a few extra doses of the antidote but asked to keep the remaining poison to work with.

Taryn agreed to her request and went to get a few hours of sleep before he and Gern set off. The coming dawn would bring a busy day with several demands, and Taryn wanted to be at his best. Bright and early, he would go to meet with Johann while Gern returned the sword to camp. Later that evening the fun would begin when Taryn would sneak back into the British camp and exchange the two swords.

Chapter Twenty-Four

The next morning was rainy so after Sarah thoroughly checked Thomas's arm and pronounced it as 'healing nicely', he and Julia began to design the fairy castle. It quickly became apparent that Thomas had grand design plans in mind and that it would take weeks, if not months, to complete the castle to his satisfaction. His enthusiasm was contagious, however, and Julia quickly became as enamored of the project as her young nephew.

When the sun broke in the early afternoon, Sarah took over with Thomas' training and together the two of them went in search of some new herbs to study. Nanny used the quiet time to retire for a short nap, while Julia set about cleaning up after the noon meal.

As she cleared the plates and utensils, Julia mused back over the story which her father had shared with Taryn. It certainly clarified some of the reasons behind Johann's past decisions and cast their father in an entirely different light. Julia realized that she too had often judged her father as weak and spineless. She was reminded once again that no human could understand the burdens another carried, and she was chagrined that she hadn't given her father the same consideration that she would have given almost anyone else. She winced as she realized that she had had the temerity to take Thomas without even considering what he might have felt, and she knew that she had some amends to make as soon as she returned home.

After fetching well water to clean the dishes, Julia also pondered the fact that Brigid mentioned Razgar to her only hours before Johann mentioned him to Taryn. Although these synchronicities were commonplace among enchanters, they always gave Julia a moment's pause and admiration for the way in which the universe worked. It truly was amazing; the signs were there if you just paid attention.

Her mind was thus engaged elsewhere when she first felt the hair on the back of her neck rise and sensed a presence in the room. She paused for a moment, turned, and surveyed the space. Nothing seemed to be amiss. She tuned in to her other knowing; there was still no forthcoming information, so she shrugged and turned back to the task at hand.

This type of thing happened fairly often. When you did the work Taryn and Julia did, you became extremely sensitive to energy shifts. Sometimes you even picked up on something insignificant such as a person who was discussing you or thinking of you strongly. The feeling generally meant little and faded away quickly. The next signal came a few moments later. As she was putting the last of the plates away, she thought that she heard her name called softly. She looked around. It had sounded like Taryn, but how could that be? He had ridden out with Gern early that morning. She must be mistaken.

Julia realized that the stress and the chaos of the last few days must be catching up with her. She decided that as soon as she was finished with her work, she would follow Nanny's excellent example and take a nap of her own.

The second time she heard her name called, she was convinced that Taryn was trying to reach her and began to build up the fire in the hearth. She needed to establish the link and find out why her brother was calling her. As Julia worked, she began to worry that something had gone terribly wrong with her antidote. She had felt some pressure to complete it as Tay was only staying the night. Although she had double-checked it, she would have felt better if she'd been able to check it again in the morning when she was fresh. But Taryn was adamant that he needed to leave at first light so she had to complete the work quickly.

The other frightening possibility was that he had decided to return the sword early and had been injured or caught. By all rights he should still be at the castle with their father, but it was just like Taryn to change plans on a whim.

Julia was so worried about her brother that she couldn't even sustain her righteous aggravation. Perhaps he had been wounded, or worse, captured. He must need her desperately if he was calling to her in the middle of the day.

She quickly sprinkled the powder into the fire. Initially the flames wavered and it appeared that an image was trying to form, but in the end, nothing solid appeared. Julia knew that the difficulty the image had forming didn't bode well for her brother's well being. If Tay were fine, the image would come in clear and strong as always. Part of what helped them connect through the firelink was their own power and energy as enchanters.

Frustrated and anxious, she tried again, sprinkling more powder into the fire and calling out desperately to her brother. This time, the colors held for a moment, then wavered in the flames, and finally began to coalesce into recognizable shapes. The place that appeared was dark around the edges of the fire, and Julia had difficulty seeing clearly. From what she could decipher, she realized it must be the inside of a tent. Julia peered intensely into the hearth trying to read more clues even as the picture grew and focused before her.

Suddenly, she gasped and stepped back as she was able to read the scene. It was an image of Taryn, beaten and bloody in the enemy camp. He was lying on the ground with his back to her and she could hear him moaning. There were two armed British guards standing over him. For a moment, she thought she saw a shadow in the far corner of the tent move, but when she looked back, there was nothing there.

Even with her dismay at seeing her brother this way, Julia's training was so well ingrained that she was studying the tent and memorizing its layout without even being consciously aware of it. This was information that she would need in order to find and rescue her brother. She also noted that the only injured man in the tent was Tay and wondered where Gern was. They would have had to kill the man to keep him from defending Taryn.

Once the link was severed, Julia's mind and body immediately went into action. Had she taken a moment to calm down, check in with her allies, or recall Brigid's warning, things might have gone differently. But she was so worried by the image of her brother in distress that all she could think of was to rush to his rescue. She rapidly began to make plans. First she summoned the Wolf and Rook and informed them of this crisis. Reggie immediately offered to fly ahead and scout out the enemy camp, but Julia was having none of that.

No, Reggie. I need you to stay with the Wolf and make sure that Thomas, Sarah, and Nanny are all safe. Since the mindlink is affected by distance, it will most likely not work for us. If something happens here, you are the one that will be able to get to me the soonest. Fly fast and let me know, and I will return with you immediately. Once I reach the camp, I am sure that the Hawk will be nearby and I will try to make contact with her. She can help me on that end if she is able. I can't help but think that something must have happened to her, or she would have flown to get us.

She may not want to leave Taryn.

That's true. I can't imagine either of you leaving me if the situation were reversed.

The Wolf piped in. **Are you sure that this is wise, Julia? It seems a bit rash to just rush off like this.**

Any moment that my brother is at the enemy's mercy is a moment too long. I clearly saw him in the link and he needs me. Now if that's everything, I must set about making my plans. Where are Thomas and Sarah?

They are deep in the woods - a good hour's walk from here.

I can't delay with a detour to tell them of my plans. I'll wake Nanny and inform her, and she can share the news with Sarah. As for Thomas, I don't want him to worry, so they can come up with a story for him.

If you're sure that we should stay here...

I'm sure, Reggie. But thanks, to you both. I'll feel better knowing that the rest of my family is safe. After I rescue Taryn, I'll send word via the Hawk that all is well.

One more thing...There has been a breech in the perimeter.

Julia was instantly on alert. *Who was it?*

A Sparrow. He flew in early this morning, a few hours after Taryn left. Wolf and I have kept an eye on him and he seems to be building a nest in one of the trees.

Julia laughed with a release of nervous energy. *A sparrow?*

Don't dismiss him too quickly. He could be an ally for someone sent to spy on us.

111

Building a nest?
What better way to appear harmless?
It's a sparrow, Reggie. Nothing could be more harmless.
Are you certain?
Don't worry. If he annoys you, you can always eat him for breakfast.

With that dismissal, Julia turned on her heel and hurried into her room. She knew that she would need a disguise and had already decided that the best one was that of a young flag bearer in the enemy's army. These boys were rarely noticed and often ignored. As such, she would be able to sneak around the camp and find her brother. If she were lucky, she might even be asked to bring food to the prisoner. She quickly created her disguise and packed her saddlebags with her healing herbs and powders. When she was ready to leave, she woke Nanny, who was startled to see a teenage lad peering at her, and explained the situation.

In a very short while, Julia was off to the stables to borrow a nag. Firefly would never do, as he was not a horse that a young flag bearer would ever be given to ride. Even though she didn't plan on riding into camp, she couldn't be sure that she wouldn't be stopped on the way there. She must be prepared for every contingency; Taryn's very life was at stake.

As Julia rode out, every ounce of her energy was focused on Taryn and the pain that he must be in. She tried to send him assurance that she was on her way, but no matter how hard she tried, she couldn't mindlink with her brother. She was petrified of losing him and pushed the horse to go faster than it ever had.

Because she had often taken flights over the battlefield with the Rook, she knew the places where both camps were located and thus the direction in which she must head. As she rode, Julia was so distracted and worried that she never even noticed the tiny Sparrow who was flying just a short distance behind her. Thankfully, the Rook did.

Chapter Twenty-Five

Taryn awoke with a start. His heart was pounding as he sat up, rubbed his hands over his face, and tried to clear his head. He noted with chagrin that the fire in the hearth had gone out, and he was surprised that he had slept so long and deeply. That wasn't like him. It must have been the wine that he and Shira had consumed with lunch.

As he looked at the beautiful woman sleeping quietly beside him, he recalled the sweet dream that he had been having only moments before. He and Shira had been in the meadow by the lake playfully teasing, kissing, and just enjoying each other's company. Suddenly, the idyllic setting had been disrupted by the sound of his sister's voice urgently calling out to him. Taryn shook his head as he realized how discordant that had been. Her tone had been insistent enough that it had awakened him even from a deep sleep. Leave it to Julia to try to disrupt his time with Shira - even in his dreams!

Taryn knew that Julia didn't like or trust Shira, and if he were honest with himself, he knew that he didn't trust her entirely either. But she was a passion that he found difficult to quell. For one thing, she was a stunning beauty, and for another, there was an element of danger about her which resonated with him. It was the same craving which was fulfilled when he was performing complex enchantment work, such as the recent theft of Carlson's sword. It made him feel excited to be alive.

Taryn was aware that he had rarely felt alive since Celia's death. In many ways, he had shut down when she died. He had spoken the truth to his father when he said that it had been Thomas who had forced him to go on living and finally heal. He knew that at some point he should look for a mother for his son, but he wasn't ready to let anyone into his heart the way that Celia had been. Her death had meant the death of a large part of him.

In the meantime, Julia was serving admirably as a maternal role model for Thomas, while Shira took consummate care of him in certain other wifely duties. Taryn was happy to sneak away and enjoy his passion with her. While she would never take the place of his beloved wife, she was an enticing distraction from the stress of war and the demands that he faced as an enchanter and healer.

Since Julia couldn't understand or support the role that Shira played in his life, he simply blocked her out when he was with Shira. That made everything much more simple and prevented Julia's interference via the mindlink. He had even blocked her today although he knew they were probably too distant for the link to work anyway.

Taryn knew that he would have to give Shira up at some point, but it would be on *his* schedule, not Julia's, and, thinking back on the pleasure of this afternoon, he knew that he would wait until it was absolutely necessary.

Much as he hated to leave, he knew that it was time to ride back to the camp and make plans to return the sword. Shira stirred as she felt her lover move from the bed. She reached out to him. "Can't you stay a little longer?"

Taryn leaned over to kiss her. "I wish I could, my love, but Gern is waiting for me at the camp. We have an important undertaking this evening."

"At least let me entice you with some more food before you leave."

He groaned with desire. "There have been enticements enough already. It's time for me to go."

As Taryn took his leave of Shira and rode to rejoin the army, he thought back happily on his fruitful day. The meeting with his father had been extremely successful; Johann had realized that the army needed to fight offensively and had given Taryn permission to truly lead the men. His afternoon with Shira had been a success of a different, yet equally enjoyable, sort. And the antidote seemed to be working; he had no more dizzy spells. As he began to look forward and plan for the evening's adventure, he realized that this was the most interesting his life had been in a long time.

Chapter Twenty-Six

By late evening, Julia was on the outskirts of the enemy camp. She stopped to drink in a stream and used the moonlight's reflection to check that her disguise was still in place. She was relieved to see that she could barely recognize herself in the shallow water. She did, indeed, look the image of a callow lad. "Well, here goes," she muttered as she made the final preparations for her entry to camp. First, she found a safe place to hide the horse and her saddlebags and then started the mile or so trek into camp. If all went well, she would return in a few hours with her brother.

Julia was amazed at how easily she walked into the enemy camp. Barely a head turned her way. It was almost as if she were invisible. She congratulated herself on the disguise and thought that if everything proceeded this way, she would ferret Tay out to safety in no time. As she walked through camp, careful to create a young lad's stride, Julia spotted the tent which she had seen in the firelink. Taryn was in there; she was sure of it.

She tried to reach into the tent with her mind and let him know that she was here. Nothing. Why couldn't she sense him? As her mind started to race with possible reasons as to why she couldn't connect with her brother, she lost her outward focus and stumbled in a rut. When she started to fall, she let out a squeal which was a bit too high-pitched even for a young boy. Several of the men looked up and one even shouted out, "Hey, lad. You sound more like a girl than a soldier!" Sounds of laughter echoed around Julia as she got up and brushed herself off.

If only they knew, Julia thought. She hung her head and smiled shyly as if in embarrassment and continued moving through the camp. Luckily, the men quickly turned back to whatever they had been doing before her fall, and she was allowed to proceed with no more interference. She would have to be more vigilant; she couldn't afford to make any more mistakes or attract any more notice.

Julia continued to walk toward the tent, still trying and still unable to sense her brother's energy. She was baffled by this as ever since their early training, they could always recognize each other's energy and feel each other's presence. The mindlink was reliable unless one purposely blocked the other or they were a great distance apart. They had even been known to awaken each other out of a deep sleep with it. There was no reason for Tay to block her now unless he was trying to protect her... or worse.

The fear that Julia had been trying to squelch invaded her mind, but she refused to let it take over; Taryn could not be dead. She would know if her brother had left the earth. Every fiber of her body would scream out. She hurried to find an alternative answer. Perhaps he was unconscious. That still wasn't ideal, but it was certainly preferable.

Julia realized that letting her thoughts run away with her was not helping the situation. She had to stay calm now; she was approaching the tent. She would need all of her resources focused on Tay and his rescue. Even if she had to carry him out, she would get him to safety.

The guards were relaxed as they saw the young flag bearer approach the tent - too relaxed. Julia wondered what her brother would do if he saw his men behaving this casually while guarding an important prisoner. She saw one of the men pull the other to the side to tell him a story and used the opportunity to slip around to the back of the tent. Once there, she lifted the edge of the tent and quietly slid under the material.

In the dim light, Julia thought she saw a figure lying on the ground. She gave her eyes a moment to adjust and then approached carefully. Suddenly, she heard a deep, unctuous voice in the far corner of the tent say, "Welcome, Julia. Nicely done." He paused and slowly clapped his hands as if applauding her performance. "Of course, we made it easy for you."

She turned toward the voice and saw a richly-robed man leaning casually against a shadow-filled corner of the tent. As he stepped into the light, she saw that he was tall and dark. His black hair was slicked back from his forehead and hung down in a thin ponytail. His slender physique did nothing to

116

undermine the aura of power which emanated from him. Even in this casual pose, Julia knew that six well-trained warriors would be no match for this man. He would make mincemeat of them in no time at all. Without a doubt in her heart, Julia knew that the man standing before her was Razgar.

She glanced over in confusion at what she earlier thought to be the sleeping figure of her brother, only to discover that it was a mound of well-placed pillows. "Where's Taryn?"

"He should be here shortly," his lips curled in a mocking grimace, "now that we have his sister as our prisoner."

Julia was stunned. She looked toward the flap of the tent and saw that the men who had been so casual about letting her sneak in were now at full attention. She had been such a fool. Julia groaned. Taryn was going to kill her!

"Make yourself at home, Julia. Feel free to eat and drink - partake of our hospitality while you can." He motioned gracefully to a tray which contained the food that he had been eating while he awaited her arrival. "Once your brother is here, things will change rapidly."

"What do you mean?"

The robed man leaned casually in the corner of the tent and shrugged calmly. His voice was smooth and studied when he spoke. "We'll kill you, of course." He let those words sink in before he continued. "That should end the war nicely. Your father will be grief-struck and will quickly give up his desire for warfare with none of his progeny left." He paused a moment and contemplated, as if he had only just remembered something; he took such pleasure in toying with her. "Ah yes, there will still be the little matter of Thomas. We will obviously have to dispose of him as well. But first things first."

"You bastard!" Julia ran at him with all of her fury.

He casually thrust his hand out and flicked his wrist, and she went soaring backward as if pulled by invisible strings. She was dumped unceremoniously on her backside. "Call me whatever you like, but you won't get near me. Your powers are no match for mine."

Razgar turned to the tent flap and raised his voice only slightly. "Guard!" The two men entered. "Take the dagger from her, and search her for other weapons." The two men complied and, finding nothing more, handed the dagger to Razgar and resumed their watch outside the tent.

Julia stood and watched as Razgar admired the weapon, running the smooth steel over his palm. "Finely made, Julia, and with the family crest on its hilt." He paused and looked her in the eyes. "I could use it to kill you now if I wanted to, but I'd rather see your brother's face while he watches you die."

The enchanter continued on with a voice that was no longer studied and smooth but had become fueled with hatred and condescension. "You two think that you are such powerful enchanters. You have far too much self-assurance and too little talent, and it has made you lazy. Lazy and sloppy. And now it will be your undoing." He paused and smiled at her mockingly. "As much fun as this has been, I must leave. I am off to set the trap for your brother. Hopefully, he will make it as easy as you have."

Razgar was moving to leave the tent when he heard her speak. "Wait."

He turned and arched an eyebrow. "What is it?"

Julia desperately wanted to stall for time while she tried to mindlink with Tay and warn him. "How did you do this? I saw Taryn. I know he was here."

"Ah yes, your precious firelink." He saw the surprise in her eyes and enjoyed the moment. "You think that it's so sacred? Once I learned of your way of communicating, it was an easy step from there."

She gasped in confusion. "But how did you discover it?"

He merely looked at her and arched an eyebrow.

"Tell me," she demanded indignantly.

"You're not giving the orders anymore. Perhaps you're a bit slow and haven't noticed who wields the power here. Let me assure you. It is I." He paused as if weighing the decision. "I'll tell you what you wish to know, because it only serves to illustrate my earlier point. You have become sloppy and arrogant." He nodded toward the cushions. "Sit down."

Julia remained standing where she was and tilted her chin in the fashion that her family and friends would have immediately recognized. Razgar recognized the defiance, too.

118

"Very well." He nodded as if her petty behavior were too demeaning for him to deal with. "The weak have to take power where they find it."

Julia could feel her ire rise as her fists clenched by her side, but she forced herself to remain calm. He was baiting her and she had already risen to the bait once. She wouldn't give him the satisfaction of doing it again, so she sweetly said, "Why don't you explain my weakness to me since you seem to be enjoying it so much."

Razgar smirked and began, "One of my men discovered the link."

Julia blinked in shock as Razgar, enjoying every moment of his recital, continued. "He's a young sentry who has not yet recognized his potential as an enchanter - I keep him close for that very reason. He saw you in the fire one evening and asked me about it. We kept watch every night after that and saw you again a few weeks later. Very sloppy work on your part, Julia." He mockingly emphasized each syllable. "Very sloppy. You should have known enough to block your transmissions."

Her surprise made her answer honestly. "We never knew they could be intercepted."

He sneered at her. "Well now you do, but it's too late, isn't it?" His voice was like silk. "Had you been more skilled, you would have realized that someone else was watching in." Julia was instantly reminded of the brief flash of another face that she had seen in the firelink on a few occasions. And of how quickly she had dismissed those interceptions.

Razgar pivoted to go, then turned back with a smug look on his face. He wasn't finished taunting her yet. "Shame on you for dismissing me and thinking that I was no threat."

"I've never dismissed you." Now she was even more confused. "I've never even met you."

He assumed Julia's posture and said in an overly bright and self-assured tone, "It's only a sparrow, Reggie. Don't worry. You can always eat him for breakfast."

Julia gasped as she recalled saying those very words in answer to Reggie's warning of the trespasser.

"We'll see who gets eaten, won't we, Julia?" And with that, he turned with a dramatic flourish of his robe and left the tent.

Chapter Twenty-Seven

Left alone, Julia could do nothing but berate herself. She was such a fool! The signs had all been right before her, and she had ignored them. She should have known when she couldn't sense Tay that he wasn't here. She had been duped so easily, and now her actions would get both her and her brother killed. And Thomas, too. Oh God, not TomCat. She had to do something. Warn Tay. But how?

Julia knew that even if she could get near a flame, which was highly unlikely, they would be watching the firelink. So that was out of the question. She quickly inventoried her other methods of connecting with Tay. When she reached the end of her list with no viable options, her anxiety level began to rise.

Grasping for answers, she thought back to her meeting with her teacher. Brigid had tried to warn her not to count too much on her tools, but what else had Brigid said? Julia paced around the tent racking her brain. "Remember your connection to all that you love." Julia immediately thought of her family and her allies. But her family was now in jeopardy thanks to her, and she had foolishly left both her allies behind. Why hadn't she listened to Reggie and let her come? Damn it! She'd never be able to mindlink with her from this distance. And she had no idea how close Skye was or even whether she could connect to Taryn's ally without his help.

Julia realized that she would have to try to mindlink with Tay again. It was her only hope... if he wasn't too far away or it wasn't too late to stop him from racing into a trap. She had to hurry. She laid down on the cushions which had earlier been arranged to look like a sleeping man and tried hard to relax her mind into the state necessary for mindlinks. It took some doing with her current level of agitation, but finally she was ready.

"Tay. Tay." She called up a clear picture of him. "TARYN, I need you." Nothing. Damn. She couldn't even sense his energy. She tried to settle in and connect once more...still nothing. Julia knew that Taryn was probably back at camp by now and that should be close enough for her to link with him - unless he was purposely blocking her. Because she could think of no reason for that, there must be something else blocking her from connecting with him. What could be powerful enough to prevent their connection?

Julia got up and began to pace around the tent. Even in her desperation to reach Tay, a part of her was intrigued by this new development. There must be a clue somewhere in this tent. Where was it? She looked around the space and saw nothing unusual; nothing seemed out of context.

It wasn't long before Julia realized that she wouldn't get anywhere using her eyes; she needed to rely on a different kind of sight. It had always helped her in the past and would hopefully help her now as well. Once again, she quieted her thoughts and tuned in to her sense of knowing.

She followed her instinct and sat in the center of the tent where she felt some subtle pulses of energy which seemed to completely surround her. It was as if she were in the center of an energy field. After a few moments of sitting quietly, she was drawn to the four corners of the tent. When she moved to the first corner, she found the answer to her question.

As Julia came to the place where a main support pole entered the earth, she saw something glowing faintly on the ground. She leaned down to get a closer look. A crystal. Something that, when programmed correctly and skillfully, was powerful enough to enhance or diffract energy. Just to be sure that she was on the right track, she checked the other corners of the tent and found crystals in all of them.

Because touching the crystals with her hands or moving them significantly could alert Razgar, Julia needed an alternative idea. One of the crystals was not wedged quite as far into the corner of the tent as the others. If she tapped the dirt around it gently with her shoe, she might be able to use the dirt to move the crystal out a scant few inches and wedge her body in between the crystal and the edge of the tent. Then she would be on the outside of the energy field and should be able to contact her brother.

Julia walked casually to the corner of the tent and quietly positioned the crystal and herself. She focused her mind and tried once more to contact Taryn.

Tay, are you there?

I'm here, Julia.

Reggie! Where are you?

I am flying above the enemy camp.

Be careful. This is a trap.

I know. I saw the sparrow fly after you and became suspicious, so I followed you here.

Thank God. You'll have to get word to Skye and Taryn immediately. They're going to use me to trap Tay. Please, Reggie - you have to warn him.

I'll fly to him now.

Julia took a few more precious minutes with the Rook to give her some vital information for Taryn and to receive assurances that the Wolf was protecting Thomas. When she was done, she gently moved away from the edge of the tent, repositioned the crystal, and smoothed down the dirt around it. If Razgar or any of his men came to check, it had to look exactly as it had before.

Just as she finished, the tent flap opened and a pleasant looking man dressed in the uniform of the British guard entered the tent. He didn't meet her eyes but went immediately to the tray of food which he began to clear.

Hoping that she might gain some information from him, Julia moved a bit closer and spoke. "Hello."

He glanced at her, gave her a brief smile and continued to work.

"I was wondering if you could wait a minute before you clear that. I wanted to pour myself a drink."

He motioned to the tray and stepped back from it. "Help yourself."

As she drank, she studied him over the rim of the cup. He was a few inches taller than she and appeared to be a few years younger. His hair was light brown and his face was open and unguarded. He didn't have the hardened air of an army veteran about him, and Julia hoped that he might be guileless enough to answer some of her questions. Perhaps she could glean some information that would help to get her out of this mess. The trick would be not scaring him away; he seemed to be a bit skittish and shy.

Julia had rarely resorted to using feminine wiles to get what she wanted; she was far too direct for that. But that didn't mean that she couldn't use them when the situation warranted. She purposely and smoothly shifted her demeanor to reflect a young and frightened woman who was out of her element. She allowed the very real fear that she was feeling to surface. Her hands started to shake and she placed the drink down on the tray. "Thank you."

As he started to clear the rest of the food away, she lightly touched the back of his hand. When he looked at her, she asked, "Please, tell me why you're doing this. Why do you want to hurt my family?"

He gently but firmly replied, "I don't want to hurt anyone." He turned away and went back to his task of placing the discarded scraps of food on the tray as he said, "I'm only following orders, ma'am."

Julia looked away in frustration as tears began to form in her eyes.

William saw them and in an attempt to lighten the mood said, "Or should I say, 'Sir'?"

"What?" Julia suddenly remembered her disguise. "Oh this." She motioned toward her clothing. "I guess it didn't work very well, did it?"

He hesitated and looked toward the flap of the tent before quietly saying, "Actually, it's a very good disguise. You would have fooled us in a moment. It's Razgar that you can't fool."

"Who *is* Razgar?"

"He is Lord Royce's enchanter. And a powerful one, too."

Julia snorted in disgust. Her earlier attempt to appear innocent and demure was forgotten. "How powerful can he be if he needed a sentry to see us in the firelink?"

William inhaled sharply. "He told you about that?"

Julia looked appraisingly at the young man before her. "It was you, wasn't it?"

"William!" The tent flap parted and Razgar appeared in the doorway. "Why aren't you at your post?"

William grabbed the tray and bowed out past Razgar as he said, "I was just clearing the food as you requested, sir."

"Well, be quick about it. There's no need for you to tarry with the enemy."

~~~~~~~~~~~~~~~~

The sorcerer watched as William left and then turned and followed him out of the tent. Razgar knew that Julia and William had not uncovered the secret in the short time that they were together, but he also knew that he must work to keep them apart lest they stumble upon it in the near future. Unlike the foolish young woman in his tent, Razgar had never underestimated his enemy. He wasn't about to begin now.

Chapter Twenty-Eight

Back at the camp, Taryn was listening with dismay to both the Rook and the Hawk. Reggie had connected with Skye earlier, and they had intercepted him as he neared the end of his ride back from the castle. He had immediately sent them out on recognizance and had waited impatiently for the information which they were now delivering.

She seems to be well thus far and is being kept in the sorcerer's tent which is by the edge of the British camp. There is a young man who takes food and water in to her and two armed guards who stand at the front of the tent. Getting to her will be difficult but not impossible.

What was she thinking? he said as his frustration mounted.

Unfortunately, when she saw you in the firelink and couldn't reach you telepathically, she assumed the worst. You know Julia; she had to ride off to the rescue immediately.

*Now **she** has to be rescued, and the sword has to be returned.* He shook his head as it reeled with the tasks before him. *Well, first things first. I have to get the sword back to Carlson before the switch is discovered. How far is the sorcerer's tent from the captain's, Skye?*

It's not too far, but it is at the swampy end of the campground making it harder to access from the outside.

Smart thinking on their part, but we can handle that. I'm afraid that I'm going to have to tell Gern what is happening so that, if need be, he can lead the situation back here. I'm not looking forward to his reaction to Julia's being taken. Taryn thought for a moment and shrugged. *Well, he has to be told, so it might as well be now. I'll need the two of you as well. Reggie, you'll fly back to Sarah's with a note. She needs to be informed. Are you absolutely sure that Thomas is safe there?*

Thomas is safe. The wolf pack are all there and they will take him into the woods at the first sign of trouble. The woods are their territory, and they can protect him there until you and Julia arrive.

Very well. I'll have to trust the Wolf while I deal with the sword and Julia.

~~~~~~~~~~~~~~~~~~~~~~

A few hours later Taryn and Gern were once more at the edge of the British camp. Taryn was in his dark clothing and was reviewing the final plans with Gern before placing the invisibility spell of the Deer on himself again.

"I tell you that I don't like it, Taryn. It's not safe for you to be in there alone."

Gern was adamant, but Taryn was equally so. "And I tell you that I will not risk you or anyone else to get Julia out of this mess." He softened his tone as he saw the man's crestfallen expression. "Gern, I need you. If something happens and Julia and I don't escape, it will be up to you to ride back to camp and plan a strategy with your fellow officers. Remember, get word to Father, get the men out, and keep Thomas safe. Only *after* that are you to attempt any kind of rescue of Julia and me."

Gern sighed but wouldn't meet his eyes. "I understand."

Taryn stared at him. "That's an order, Gern."

Gern looked up and met his eyes, but his response was dejected. "Yes, sir."

~~~~~~~~~~~~~~~

Upon entering the British camp, Taryn noticed that there had been a change in the energy from that of the night before. He could feel the excitement in the air even though it was after midnight and several of the men slept. Having Julia as a prisoner was a major coup for the British, and he started to worry about what they may be doing to wrest information from her.

Quickly, he realized the futility of this line of thought and forced his mind to focus first on the task at hand: the return of the sword which he had hidden under his cloak. Slowly and softly he crept toward Carlson's tent. As he approached, he saw a dim light shining from the tent and heard voices from inside.

127

"Of course he will attempt to rescue his sister. The two fools are devoted to each other. Besides, his ego alone won't allow us to keep his sister."

"I hope you're right, Razgar."

"Trust me, Carlson. I have been studying these two for years. I know exactly how they will behave in any situation. They are boringly predictable."

"If they were so easy to predict, why did you feel that Taryn would make a move for the sword? It seems that he has proven you wrong on at least that count."

"I admit that I am surprised by that. A little birdie told me that he would attempt to steal it." He paused for a moment. "You are certain that it is still here?"

"It is. I had it out earlier this evening."

"And you have it well hidden?"

"Just as we discussed - nothing too obvious."

"Good. Knowing the fool that he is, he will try for the sword and his sister at the same time."

Carlson looked with disdain at the man standing before him. He didn't like or trust Razgar, but for now, he needed him. His tone reflected this. "You can assure me that he will get neither I hope."

"I can."

"Good. I'm going to take one last walk around the camp and then I'd like you to take me to the prisoner. I need to see this headstrong child of the enemy for myself."

"I don't think you'll be very impressed." Razgar spoke drolly, as he looked at his well-manicured fingernails. "I am far from overwhelmed myself." He moved to the flap of the tent as Taryn melded into the shadow. "Shall we?" he said as he motioned to the exit.

As Taryn watched the two men leave, he realized that he was really going to need all of his skills to get out of this situation. The enemy was more prepared than he expected. He wondered why Razgar had been studying Julia and him for years. Had he, like Johann, been unable to forget the past or let it go? Had he been plotting revenge for all of these years? Taryn shook his head to clear it and focused on the return of the sword. One thing at a time. It wouldn't be long before the men finished their walk and visit to Julia, so he needed to act now.

Once again, he went into the tent through a rear corner. This time, he immediately sensed that his decoy sword was in a different position. It resided under the sleeping pillows and blankets. He quickly checked for traps and finding none, traded the two swords. He noticed almost immediately that the cloaking spell was beginning to weaken. As he looked at the decoy, its image would momentarily wobble and blur and then stabilize. He was not a moment too soon. He was only glad that Razgar had not asked to see the sword, as the wizard would have immediately recognized the deception.

He hastily withdrew his oils and smoothed them on the decoy. It was imperative that he remove the cloaking spell fully lest he be caught holding this sword when he tried to rescue Julia. If all else failed, he wanted Gern and his officers to have a fighting chance against Carlson. The only way that would happen was if no one discovered that the spell placed on the original sword had been removed. Being caught with an identical sword or worse, a sword that was morphing back and forth, would immediately place suspicion on the original.

Taryn watched as the decoy sword changed before his eyes. Once again it appeared in its original form. It was a clean, finely-made but plain silver sword. Just the kind of sword that he would carry. He strapped it on and prepared to leave the tent when he heard a commotion outside. It seemed to come from across the way and he listened as the noise became louder.

"Fire! Fire!" He heard men take up the cry as they rushed to find water.

Taryn risked peering outside and saw a large tent near the swamp engulfed in flames. He chuckled to himself as he realized what had happened; Julia had set the tent on fire. Even though this had temporarily ruined his plan to rescue her now, he had to give his sister credit. She had let the British know in no uncertain terms that she wasn't going to be held prisoner easily. And she had also let her brother know that she was still in fighting form, and that was a good sign.

Taryn and Julia had a long history of working with fire; it was a powerful ally of theirs. While initially they had discovered that the fire would facilitate communication between them, that had turned out to be only the beginning. As they became teenagers and experimented even more, they realized that they could use a flame from a candle or a spark from two rocks to create and sustain a brief flame in the palm of their hands. When they really focused, they could build the flame in their hands and then shoot or throw it some distance. Because of their competitive nature, they had often practiced "flame-throwing" as Taryn had dubbed it and had become quite good at it. They hadn't had much need for it lately, but it seemed that Julia was still in fighting practice.

Taryn watched Razgar's tent as it was fully engulfed and gave a quiet cheer for his sister even as he heard Skye's warning cry above him. He needed to act fast as more and more men were awakening every moment. Soon the entire camp would be up and he might be discovered.

Making a hasty but necessary decision, he abandoned the sword by the inner side wall of the tent and shapeshifted into a hawk. As he left and flew upwards, he looked down to see Julia being roughly pulled in the direction of Carlson's tent. He only hoped that if any of them were to discover the discarded sword, it would be Julia. Perhaps she would sense that it was the decoy; then she would know that her brother had been here once and was coming back for her.

Chapter Twenty-Nine

Julia heard the Hawk's cry but was too busy struggling with her guards to pay attention. She had managed to get a swift kick off in the direction of a shin, but they had quickly switched to pulling her from behind. And none-too-gently, either.

She heard Razgar swearing and pushing the men to get the fire out, but she herself could see that it was too late to rescue any of Razgar's belongings. She only hoped that all of his potions and medicines had been in the tent too.

Suddenly she was roughly thrust into another large tent. She fell to her knees with a shout of pain and surprise. No sooner had she stood up and started to brush herself off than a furious Razgar stormed in.

"So, this is what I get for my hospitality, Julia?"

"If that's what you call hospitality, I'd just as soon pass."

"Trust me. You don't want to wear out your welcome. You won't like your other options."

"You don't scare me, Razgar. Just because you have the power now doesn't mean you'll win. Taryn will find a way to get me out of here."

"I wouldn't count on it. Your brother is going to be very busy leading the army and protecting his son. You'll be far down on his list. He won't have much extra time for you."

"You don't know anything about my brother, so don't pretend that you do."

Razgar's eyes glittered in the light as his demeanor shifted. She might have thrown him off his game temporarily, but when it came to this, he knew that he was in the position of power. He took his time responding to her, playing out the moment when she would realize how well he had laid his trap. "That's where you're wrong, Julia. I know a great deal about you and your brother. Your entire family, in fact."

"I know that you blame Father for your son's death, but he didn't kill him."

131

Razgar shrugged; her argument carried no weight. "He was leading the army, and that makes him responsible. He will pay."

Julia reacted with all of the outrage that she felt. "You don't think killing my mother and baby brother is payment enough?"

Razgar studied her for a moment in surprise. "I wondered if Johann had pieced together the clues. I'm happy to hear that he did. I wanted him to know it was me." He paused before continuing on. "And no, I don't think that's enough. My son was my legacy in this world. I will only be happy when I have taken the same from Johann." He spoke the final words, pausing and placing emphasis on each. "Every - last - one - of - you."

Julia was quiet as she contemplated the man before her and truly saw him for the first time. She felt his drive to destroy her family and recognized his determination to succeed. Every level of her being became aware that he not only meant what he said, but that he had been carefully and methodically planning this for a long time. She was also painfully aware that he might have the skills to carry out his plan.

Julia felt an instinctive shift in herself which she didn't entirely understand. This was an enemy that she had never faced before. His abilities were on a higher, more complex level than any she had known. Her body, mind and training were all responding intuitively; she only hoped it would be enough.

She spoke in a haughty tone intended to irritate her captor and goad him into revealing more than he'd intended. "And how are you going to accomplish this, Razgar? If you have been studying us as you say, then you know that my brother and I are not totally defenseless against sorcery."

"Clearly, my tent is proof of that," Razgar replied sarcastically. "But enjoy your moment while you have it as you won't have another. I will be certain to have your hands tied whenever you are alone in the tent. As for your supposed other talents as enchanters, they're nothing to me. Notice how easily I trapped you. Taryn will only be a bit more of a challenge. Nothing much, really."

"I've been watching you and your brother for years, and I know your strengths and weaknesses. I know that you're the one who does almost all of the protection work; Taryn prefers to trust in his instincts and abilities. I know that Taryn takes more chances and often accomplishes more; you work at a slow, thoughtful pace to get where you're going, but are often more prepared for contingencies. Taryn tends to shapeshift; you use disguise. Taryn chooses confrontation; you choose stealth. Oh yes," he paused and stared at her, "Taryn is the Hawk, and you are the Rook." He laughed at her startled reaction. "You think your love for each other makes you strong, but you're wrong. I only have to knock one of you down and all of you will tumble. That's what comes from being interdependent, Julia. You are only as strong as your weakest link." Clearly, he was enjoying the moment, and couldn't resist adding silkily, "And look who that turned out to be."

Julia was flabbergasted. The man seemed to have glimpsed into their psyches. He knew their personalities, their penchants, **and** their allies. He made his next statement at the same moment as it popped into her head. "You, on the other hand, know nothing of me. You didn't even know enough to realize that your destruction of the tent was only an annoyance. Everything I need is safely put away. Except one last item." With that, he reached under the pillows and withdrew the ruby-encrusted sword.

Julia gasped as she recognized the sword. Luckily, Razgar misinterpreted her gasp of recognition as one of admiration. "Yes. It is a beauty, isn't it? I am quite proud of this fine piece of work."

As Razgar spoke, he turned the sword over in his hands admiring the workmanship. Julia studied him, looking for a sign that he knew about the work she had done on the sword, but he didn't give her one. She wondered which sword Razgar was holding - the original or the duplicate. Was it even possible that Tay had already returned the original? If not, the spell would be wearing off by now and the deception was sure to be uncovered.

Her thoughts were interrupted by the sorcerer. "Now, if you would be so kind as to sit in the corner, I will send the

133

guards in to watch you while William removes the Captain's belongings. He is perfectly happy to stay in his mistress's tent for the evening. Tomorrow, after your brother arrives, we'll move you to other accommodations. I'm afraid they won't be half as nice as my tent, but then, that's not my fault, is it?"

Julia moved to sit in the corner of the tent. "I'm sure you don't think any of this is your fault, Razgar."

"Quite the contrary. I'm perfectly willing to take credit for the destruction of Johann's lineage." With that, Razgar smiled at her, turned, and left the tent.

Chapter Thirty

While one of the guards stood watch outside, the other came and stood inside the tent flap and watched while the man named William stacked up Carlson's belongings. Julia sat watching and replaying in her mind the exchange that she had just had with Razgar. Her earlier outrage and indignation were now surpassed by her fear.

This man was a talented sorcerer, and it appeared that he intended to destroy her family. She had to think of how she could get word to Tay. Together they would come up with a way out of this situation. While her mind was ferreting out a plan, her eyes were furtively casting about the tent looking for anything she might use to aid in her escape. Suddenly a glimmer caught her eye. There was something silver just at the left side of the tent. It was barely visible as it had been shoved under the material at the edge of the tent wall. Julia turned her head in another direction so as not to draw attention to the object. She desperately prayed it would turn out to be something useful.

She decided her best course was to distract William and the guard as much as she possibly could lest they begin to look around the tent for more objects to move to Carlson's temporary quarters. She stood and moved slowly toward William. When he glanced up, she asked, "How long have you been in the army?"

"Why?"

"I'm wondering how old you are."

The young man paused, puzzled by the seemingly random question. He thought for a moment, and when he didn't see anything wrong with answering it, he did. "Eighteen."

"Have you been in the army long?"

"No, ma'am."

"Clearly your speech marks you as Scottish."

"True."

"Then why would you join the British and fight against us?"

He hesitated, shrugged, and then said, "Lord Razgar came to my house and asked my mother to send me to help him fight."

Julia was puzzled by this. It made no sense. Why would an enchanter recruit a common guard? "Did Razgar do this with many others?"

William blushed. "No, ma'am. It appears he knew my mother a long time ago, and she owed him a debt."

The other guard, discomforted by the conversation without knowing why, interrupted. "Are you almost done?"

"Almost. You can take that pile to the woman's tent if you'd like. I'll stay here and finish up. When you return, I'll take the final pile."

The guard hesitated. He didn't want to risk Razgar's wrath by leaving, but it seemed like a fairly safe situation to him. There was still one guard outside the tent, and William was inside with the prisoner. She would be watched the entire time and all William would have to do was yell and the guard outside would come right in. Selfishly, he was also thinking that all of the women's tents were grouped in the same area, and perhaps, he could sneak in a few moments with his wife after he delivered the clothes to Carlson's mistress.

Julia, seeing his hesitation, offered a seemingly perfect solution. "Since Razgar wants my hands tied when you both leave, why don't you do it now? Then you can be sure that I won't do any harm."

The guard, only too willing to take the way out that Julia offered, quickly tied her hands and grabbed the pile of clothing. Julia and William could hear him conversing briefly with the guard on outside duty and whistling as he set off for the women's camp.

William looked at her tentatively. "That was nice of you."

"What was?"

"Offering to have your hands tied so we could finish up more quickly here."

"My hands are tied in more ways than this I'm afraid." She lifted them from where they were tied against her back.

The young man hesitated, then said, "I'm sorry."

Julia heard the sincerity in the tone. "I believe you." She watched him as silence hung in the air. "You're just caught up in this whole war like the rest of us. It isn't any of your doing."

William's emotions were barely repressed as he replied, "I hate it. I hate the idea of killing people, especially fellow Scots. I wish I were back in the Highlands with my mother." He hung his head, embarrassed by his outburst. "It's just that I...I don't know how she is coping without me."

Despite her own worries, Julia found herself caught up in this young man's tale. "What do you mean? I'm sure she misses you, but she must have someone else there to help her."

"No, there's no one." The dam broke and the worries that had been eating at William spilled out. "My father died when I was a baby, and it's only been the two of us since then. Now, she's trying to run an entire farm by herself. Lord Razgar sends men to help at harvest time, but at all the other times, it's just us. I would never have come if Mother hadn't insisted. She said that we owed a great deal to Razgar, and it was my duty to fulfill our debt." He looked at Julia in frustration. "What debt? What debt could poor farmers possibly owe to a sorcerer like Lord Razgar?"

Julia was thoughtful. There was something more to this story. She felt it but couldn't identify what it might be. What debt could William and his mother possibly owe to Razgar? Julia didn't know the answer yet, but she hoped for William's sake that Razgar was finished collecting his payment.

Once William had taken the final pile of clothing out of the tent, Julia made a few quick decisions. The first was to keep her hands tied. She could easily get out of the ropes that were binding her but didn't want to tip her hand on that score. She knew at some point she would need to be free; now was not the time.

Her second decision was to wait until the guard thought that she was asleep before going over to explore the silver metal object that she had seen glinting by the side of the tent. She lay down on the cushions and tried to get comfortable with her hands tied. She relaxed her mind which was racing with all of the possible scenarios for escape. Before she could unravel which were the best strategies, the events of the past few days and the late hour caught up with her, and she fell fast asleep.

Chapter Thirty-One

Taryn was far from sleep as he huddled with Gern and his officers in his tent making plans for the coming evening.

"I think the best thing for us to do is to attack and try to rescue Julia at the same time. That way, Carlson's men will be occupied, and there will be less chance of interference in the rescue."

Gern piped up. "I agree, and I volunteer to go into the camp to rescue your sister."

"No, I will rescue Julia. I won't have any of the rest of you put yourselves in harm's way."

One of his senior officers cleared his throat. "Begging your pardon sir, but this is a war we are fighting. It would seem that we are **all** in harm's way."

Taryn's jaw tightened with frustration. "Yes, James, you are correct, of course, but I still insist that I be the one to infiltrate the camp. I've already done so on two occasions, so I know the layout better than anyone else."

Even Gern couldn't find an argument for that, so he said, "I still think that you should take at least one man with you to guard your back."

"I can't spare any of you, and it will be easier for me to work alone." He looked around the makeshift table at the silent men before him. "Now that **that's** settled, let's focus on the plan for your attack. We only have a couple of hours left before dawn and we need some sleep before we launch our plan later tonight." With those words, the men huddled over the roughly drawn maps which were spread out before them and devised a strategy that they felt had a good chance of success.

It was almost sunrise when the meeting concluded, and the officers left Taryn's tent to catch a few hours of sleep before the long day and night that lay ahead. Gern hesitated in the entrance to the tent. Taryn could feel the man's frustration and hastened to speak first. "Gern, I know that you would rather be with me rescuing Julia, but you are a strong fighter and swordsman. I need you at the battlefront."

"But..."

"No buts about it, Gern. I'll be fine. And so will Julia. I'll bring her back safe and sound."

Gern took one look at his boss and knew that he would brook no more arguments. And so it was a dejected man who mumbled, "Yes, sir," as he left and let the tent flap fall closed behind him.

~~~~~~~~~~~~~~~

Once Taryn was alone, he began to move quickly. He had an agenda that he had shared with no one until now, but it was time. He gathered his belongings and left the camp grounds for a clearing that he knew of in the forest. It was imperative that he speak with Skye and Reggie; he wanted to get their input and support and check on whether they had any updates on Julia and how she was faring on enemy turf. He would need the most current information available before he left on this early morning mission.

Chapter Thirty-Two

Back in the British camp, William was standing a lonely guard duty by the swamp and mulling over the strange occurrences of the past few days. He had finally met the enemy that they had been fighting for weeks. Or at least the daughter of the enemy.

He smiled as he thought of the feisty, outspoken woman in Carlson's tent. She wasn't anything like he had imagined. In fact, if William were honest, he liked Julia. And the more he learned about her, the more he respected her as well. She must be frightened to death for herself and her family, and yet she had handled this whole situation extremely well. That was more than he could say for Razgar. Far more.

He couldn't understand why his mother was so loyal to the man; he had yet to find one positive attribute that Razgar displayed. In fact, he had never liked him and had always dreaded his visits to the farm. Luckily, they were infrequent, as they left both him and his mother moody and restive for a few weeks afterwards. Even though he had inquired about their connection, his mother had remained strangely silent on the topic. Perhaps she would finally tell him when he returned home.

As his thoughts turned to the beauty of his home in the Highlands, he realized he was also finding much to appreciate here in the south of Scotland. True, the Scottish territory that he had recently seen was not on the ocean like his home, but it offered its own scenic vistas - miles of lush green land spread out before him. Of course, that wasn't the case right now. All that spread out before him now was the swamp to his right and one broiled tent to his left.

William looked at the damage that Julia had caused to Razgar's tent, and he had to smile; he admired her courage. He didn't think anyone would ever dare to purposely anger Razgar, but now that he had met Julia, he knew that the camp sorcerer had a serious battle on his hands. William could only wonder what Julia's brother was like. He realized with surprise that he was almost looking forward to meeting him.

~~~~~~~~~~~~~~~~

Skye clutched the helpless mouse in her talons. He was hanging from her claws and dangling precariously. She wondered why he wasn't more frightened. She would be if the roles had been reversed.

As she flew over the territory on the edge of the British camp, she accidentally dropped the mouse before she was ready. She watched as he bounced off a pile of hay and scurried to safety among all of the tents in the camp. Darn. She would have to keep an eye out and watch for an opportunity to grab that mouse again.

~~~~~~~~~~~~~~~~

Julia was awakened by a small cheeping noise in her ear. She opened her eyes and saw a tiny mouse before her. She studied it intently for a few moments listening to the noise it made and then sprang into action as the mouse hurried from the tent.

The first thing that Julia did was to check the silver object which she had seen glinting along the side of the tent the night before. It was a plain silver sword. Just the type of sword her brother would use to carry a cloaking spell. She used her feet to shuffle more rocks and dirt over the sword so that it would remain hidden from view. She may need it in the near future.

The next thing that Julia did was to check the Captain's tent for crystals to see whether any attempt at communication with her brother or allies would be blocked. Although she saw no evidence of that, when she tried to mindlink with Taryn, Reggie, or Skye, nothing came through. Frustrated, she tried to determine what was interfering. Although she walked the tent perimeter, still she saw nothing that would impede her ability to mindlink.

Just as she was about to try to get through to the Rook once more, she heard a commotion outside of the tent. The entrance flap was hastily thrown to one side, and Razgar

142

entered holding a small cage. It contained the tiny mouse that had just visited Julia. She paled when she saw the creature trying frantically to break free from his prison.

Razgar held the cage before her allowing it to dangle from one finger and swing precariously back and forth. "Really Julia, you and your brother underestimate me. I have known for years that one of his favorite strategies is shapeshifting. Did you think I wouldn't watch for it? You both are far too predictable, always resorting to the same tired strategies and skills."

Julia bluffed. "I don't know what you're talking about Razgar. As far as I can see all you have is a mouse in a cage."

"Oh, is that all? Well then, let me feed him to my cat."

Still desperately trying to win the bluff, she said, "Why are you here? Dawn has barely broken. So you caught a mouse. Couldn't that news wait for later in the day, or do you really have that little in your life to interest you?"

Razgar narrowed his eyes as he looked at Julia. "Don't try to fool me. You know damn well who I have in this cage."

She spit out, "Then let him go. It's no fun to torture a mouse. Wouldn't you rather have the man?"

Razgar knew, as did Julia, that Taryn was unable to use any of his powers when he was in a different form. He had all of the abilities of the animal form he was in and his human intellect, but that was as far as it went. He retained one other ability, and that was to shapeshift back into his human form. And he couldn't do that without the room to grow, something that the tiny cage was preventing him from doing.

Razgar contemplated Julia's question. She did have a good point; it was more fun to torture a man, especially this man. But the timing wasn't quite right. He made his decision. "Not yet. I think that I'm going to keep him a mouse for a while longer." He smiled at Julia as he swung the cage back and forth. "But don't worry. I'll let him watch you and Thomas die as a man."

Razgar left the tent accompanied by an epithet from Julia and the squeals of a very angry mouse.

Chapter Thirty-Three

When Gern arose late the next morning, he went to find Taryn. Now that they had all had some sleep, he was more determined than ever to convince the man that his plan to rescue Julia all by himself was foolhardy. There were plenty of fine officers who could lead the army while Gern went with Taryn and covered his back. And, of course, Gern was also anxious to assure himself of Julia's safety. When he thought of Julia being trapped in the enemy camp, Gern became filled with a degree of rage that he had only rarely experienced before. He swore that if even one hair on her head had been harmed, there would be hell to pay. And Gern would personally deliver the bill.

Gern reached Taryn's tent and immediately noticed that it looked just as they had left it the night before. It didn't appear that Taryn had even slept here. As Gern continued to look around, he developed a feeling in the pit of his stomach that he didn't much like; it told him that something had gone wrong. Damn it! Obviously, the fool had gone off and tried to rescue his sister early.

As tempted as Gern was to rush in after Taryn, he knew that he needed to keep a cool head. No matter what he personally wanted, he had to stay with the army and lead them in through the swamp. After the battle was fought, successfully he hoped, he would find Taryn and Julia and rescue them. In the meantime, he had to make sure that everything was ready for tonight's attack. It was up to him now.

~~~~~~~~~~~~~~~

Back in Carlson's tent, Julia was also making plans for this evening's attack. At least she had managed to learn about that from her brother before Razgar captured him. It had now been several hours since she had seen either Tay or Razgar and Julia wondered what was keeping the latter away. She fervently hoped that he wasn't busy torturing her brother, or worse, going after Thomas, but she also realized that there was

144

no more time to waste worrying or being angry or frustrated. She was focusing all her energy on devising a way out of this situation.

She reviewed all that she knew about Razgar. Clearly, he had been studying her and her brother for quite some time and knew a great deal about their skills. And yet, he hadn't expected the fireball which Julia had thrown at his tent. He also didn't seem to realize that Julia could easily escape the ropes he had tied around her hands. Why was that? Had his much vaunted research been incomplete?

It didn't take long for Julia to realize that Razgar didn't know any of the talents that she and Taryn hadn't used in the past several years. Both the flame throwing and bond removal were lessons from their youth. Neither had had to employ them in recent years, so Razgar hadn't witnessed their use.

Sure that she had stumbled on a key, Julia forced herself to think of all of the skills that Taryn and she had honed as children and had abandoned for more practical techniques once they had become healers. It was only a short while later when Julia smiled to herself. She recognized the solution: a way that she and Tay might be able to get out of this mess. If only she could get word to her brother.

~~~~~~~~~~~~~~~

Meanwhile a very unhappy mouse was pacing his small cage. How the hell had Razgar spotted him? Taryn had thought that shapeshifting into a mouse was a perfect cover. He had never become a mouse before, but they were small and plentiful in this part of the land. And yet, Razgar had been waiting and watching for him. Taryn realized that in some ways, Razgar was correct - both he and Julia always reverted to form. Like most humans, they fell into patterns, always choosing the skills that they were strongest in when under duress or threatened. Maybe the trick was for him and Julia to do something totally unpredictable. Something Razgar would never expect from either of them... but what could that possibly be?

Chapter Thirty-Four

Razgar regretted that he had to spend the day away from his prisoners, but his current mission was one of extreme importance to the overall plan. He was laying the groundwork for the crowning moment when Johann was killed by his own son. And just in case something went awry with his prisoners and they escaped, he would make sure that they were also part of the familial slaughter. Razgar congratulated himself on his cleverness. No one would ever suspect what was to come. He had kept this part of the plan to himself, trusting no other until today.

As much as he hated to share his secrets, Razgar knew that there was one person he would have to trust. Indeed, he must have an ally in order to carry this final glorious moment out. Even a talented sorcerer could only be so many places at once and the timing of this sequence of events must be impeccable.

Razgar had played and replayed every detail of his revenge over and over in his mind, looking for flaws and weaknesses. It was this part in particular that had occupied much of his time and energy. Johann's son was a young man who was not prone to rash action; therefore, he must be provoked beyond all reason. After much thought, Razgar had found a way to do just that. It was slightly regrettable, and he had tried to avoid it, but the sacrifice must be made. He had given her so much. Now it was time to collect his payment. Razgar knew that he must triumph at all costs.

Chapter Thirty-Five

By late afternoon Julia realized that she could no longer waste time planning a strategy or trying to mindlink with Tay or her allies. There must be a crystal somewhere in here preventing it, and the time for action was now. Razgar could stop her from contacting her allies in this reality, but he couldn't stop her from contacting them in other realities.

The reason that Julia had delayed working in the other reality was that it didn't always translate directly to this one. For example, time there was not directly equitable to time here and now. The animal allies or a teacher might say something would happen "soon" and it could be a few months before it occurred in day-to-day reality. Also messages tended to come in codes which were similar to those employed in dreams. They were layered in metaphor or symbols which often took time to decipher. For these reasons and more, when in immediate danger, she tried to work in the reality where the danger existed. Julia didn't see that as an option right now, so she did the next best thing.

She lay down and quieted her mind, slowed her breathing rate, and adjusted her body to the trance state necessary to journey into what was known as the lower world. As she felt herself relax, she set her intention to meet the Wolf, the Rook and Taryn in Brigid's clearing. She pictured herself stepping out of her body, walking through the mist, and descending to the lower world where Brigid's clearing and her allies would be waiting.

The Rook spoke first. **Welcome, Julia. We've been waiting for you.**

I'm happy to see you both and know that you're fine. Wolf, how is Thomas?

He's safe. No one has bothered us.

Good, but please don't let your guard down. Razgar is bent on the destruction of our family and Thomas is an important part of our future.

He'll be safe, Julia. But what about you? How can we help you?

First things first. Can you please untie these ropes?
Lie down and we'll begin.

Julia lay on the pine needle-covered ground in Brigid's clearing and closed her eyes as the Wolf and Rook chewed and struggled with the bonds that tied her. She worked her hands back and forth to help slacken the ropes. Finally she felt them loosen and knew that she was free.

As she got back on her feet, she heard a noise and saw her brother appear in the clearing. The siblings hugged each other and then immediately began to plan. There wasn't a moment to waste.

I'm telling you, Tay, I can make this work.

You haven't done this in years. Taryn looked doubtful.

That's the beauty of it. Razgar knows nothing about this. And it fits perfectly with your idea.

True. Razgar will never expect you to be the one who acts and me to be the one who does the quiet work.

Right. We'll fool him on two fronts. Also, don't forget what Brigid said to me. 'Trust what you know in your heart to be true.' What I know to be true is that Razgar's wrong. Our love doesn't make us weak; it makes us strong - stronger than any outside threat.

That may be true, but don't underestimate the power of Razgar's hatred.

I'm not, but I really think this is the key. She was one of my most powerful allies when I was a child.

Taryn thought for a minute. *Very well, Julia. You may be right. It's our best option right now. You act and I will provide the energy cover. I can do that from here and not be hindered by my shape as a mouse.*

How much time do you need before I can begin?

Give me an hour.

Is that enough?

It'll have to be.

The siblings hugged each other and took their leave. When Julia felt herself return to her physical body in Carlson's tent, she immediately removed the ropes which were now loosely hanging off her hands and began to arrange the items in the tent to suit her needs. She had one hour to prepare - a

148

far shorter amount of time than she would like, but it would have to do. She was so caught up in her preparation that she never even heard a sound until he spoke.

"What do you think you're doing?"

She turned to see a guard holding a food tray and standing in the doorway. He noticed her untied hands and muttered a curse. "How did you get free?"

Julia thought fast. "Razgar had me untied just now because he knew that you had gone to fetch my dinner. He said that you could retie me when I finish eating."

She held her breath as the guard seemed to ponder her words. Finally, perhaps because he could see no other viable explanation, he accepted her words as true.

"All right. I didn't realize that he was back yet. Here's your food." He placed the tray on a large trunk. "I'll return shortly to see that you've eaten and to retie your hands. Don't try anything or this will be the last meal that you get."

"Don't worry. I'm very hungry. I'll behave myself, I promise." She gave him her most beguiling smile which earned her a growl and grimace as he turned and left the tent.

Julia didn't even look at the food. There was no time for that now. She couldn't even give Tay his full hour to prepare. She had to act fast, before the guard came back to retie her hands and Razgar returned from wherever he had been.

She stood in the center of the tent and noted the four directions around her. She called in the energy of the four quadrants, apologizing for her neglect over the past few months and begging their assistance at this critical time. She explained that the work was not only to benefit her; it would also help her nephew who was sure to be a future healer and was already showing promise in honoring and working with Nature.

Julia took her time with her request. She knew that paying homage was not something to be rushed, no matter how urgent her need might feel. When she felt ready, she stepped purposely into the northern quadrant of the wheel.

Chapter Thirty-Six

William was once again stationed as a sentry by the swamp entrance to the camp. He looked about wondering why anyone would even attempt an attack from this end of the camp when there were so many other more suitable ways to approach. He sighed, shifted into a more comfortable position, and supposed he should be happy that he had a nice quiet spot to guard. As long as that damn bird didn't come back, things should remain peaceful.

The sun was just in the final moments of setting when he noticed that there was still a faint glow from it over in the distant corner of the swamp. Having nothing better to occupy his time, he wondered in fascination how the last of the sun's rays might reflect that type of light in only one specific area. As he absentmindedly looked in that direction, he saw the glow appear to bob up and down slightly. That was odd. Perhaps that wasn't the setting sun after all, but what else could it be? Was there someone out there in the distance?

For a moment, William wondered if he should alert any of the other guards. Then he realized how ridiculous that would seem if it were just the setting sun reflecting off a surface. He decided just to watch the light for a while and see if it moved again.

~~~~~~~~~~~~~~~

What William didn't know was that he was watching the light of a steadily advancing army. Taryn and his officers had decided to use the British plan to attack through the dried out swamp against them. They were sure that the British were arrogant enough to believe that they were the only ones who could come up with such a plan and would therefore leave this entrance only lightly guarded.

The only reason Gern was even allowing one light during the stealthy advance was because the dried out swamp had some rather large crevices and deep damp areas that they were hoping to avoid. He had draped the light with a piece of

150

material to dull the glow, but he still feared that a watchful sentry might be alerted to the army's approach. They would all have to hope that the heavens were on their side this evening, and that the sentries were sleeping off their evening meal.

Gern had moved the plan up from a midnight attack to sunset because he feared that any more time wasted might be a threat to the well being of Taryn and Julia. And Gern was determined to do all that he could to assure their safety.

~~~~~~~~~~~~~~~

William realized that the last of the sun's rays had now completely set. The light he was seeing could not be the sun but had to be a light that someone was holding. Someone who was sneaking up to the edge of the British camp. He hurried to alert his fellow soldiers before it was too late.

~~~~~~~~~~~~~~~

From his position near the front of the line, Gern was sure that he saw a shadow hurrying off from the top edge of the swamp. He knew that was a bad sign and was damned if one man was going to spoil the plans of an entire army.

He spoke briefly with a fellow officer and stole silently into the shadows to intercept the man. He had to stop the guard from alerting the British when they were still this far out. This attack had to be flawless. It was life or death for all of them.

~~~~~~~~~~~~~~~

The Hawk and the Rook watched from above as William and Gern both snuck off. They could see what was happening below and immediately corrected their flight to intercept the British guard. Since they couldn't help either Julia or Taryn at the moment, they would do the next best thing and help Gern.

~~~~~~~~~~~~~~~

Gern took a moment to bend down and pick up the thick branch that he had just stumbled on. If he couldn't get close enough to use his sword, he could always hurl the branch at the running figure of the guard once he got closer. Even if it only tripped him or slowed him down, it might buy Gern enough time to get to the man and stop him permanently.

He gripped the thick branch tighter as he raced through the swamp heedless of his own safety. He would never catch up with the sentry unless Providence smiled on him. Gern swore as he ran hoping that Providence was indeed on their side and smiling. At least one thing was in his favor. The wind had started to whip up and would cover some of the noise of the army's movement as they approached the encampment.

~~~~~~~~~~~~~~~~

William didn't know that Gern was after him, but he did know that this was turning into a very strange night. The wind was starting to really howl and every time he neared the end of the path that opened into the camp, two large birds would fly at him and squawk. He didn't know why but he couldn't get past them. He tried to shoot them down with the arrows he had, but the wind was making a true aim very difficult. Why were the birds attacking him? Was he near a nest? If so, why hadn't this ever happened before?

He tried shouting, but no one in camp could hear him over the wind. William couldn't believe that he was unable to raise the alarm or attract anyone's attention. What would the legends say about the British if they were undone by a few birds and some wind? Even in the heat of the moment, he realized how absurd that was. He ran to try another path into the camp. It might take a few minutes more, but right now, it was the best option that he could find.

~~~~~~~~~~~~~~~~

Julia could feel when the wind moved one of the heretofore undiscovered crystals and freed her from the energy bonds which Razgar had put in place. She immediately

152

mindlinked with her brother and saw what he was doing. It was a good idea and she hoped it would work. In the meantime, she had her hands full trying to hold up her end of the plan. But she did manage to contact Reggie and let her know what her brother was up to. Maybe she and Skye could help Tay.

~~~~~~~~~~~~~~~~

Razgar, who was in the tent he had commandeered from an officer, was wallowing in the brilliance of his machinations. He had just returned to camp a few minutes earlier and didn't take much notice of the wind at first, but when it really started to howl, he turned his attention to it. Something about this wind and its sudden occurrence didn't feel entirely natural.

He looked over at the small mouse in the cage and noticed that it was quiet - asleep in a corner. No problem there. Not that he thought there would be. What, after all, could a mouse do?

He also knew that Julia was helpless - her power was contained by the crystals which he had placed outside of her tent. They had been carefully programmed to block all of her specific skills including the newly discovered ability to work with fire. This time, he knew better than to place them inside the tent. Actually, even Julia's earlier discovery of the crystals had worked to his advantage. She had drawn her brother right into the trap and saved Razgar the trouble of devising his own plan to lure Taryn to the camp.

As Razgar absent-mindedly ate the grapes on the tray before him, he went back to his self-congratulatory thoughts. He almost regretted how easy this had all been. Almost, not quite.

~~~~~~~~~~~~~~~~

The Wind whispered to the cooking Fires that had been lighted all over the camp for the dinner hour. The two ancient allies came up with a plan which they undertook immediately. These two had always worked extremely well together - feeding off one another until they were almost unstoppable.

153

Tay sensed when the contact he had been working to encourage had been made and knew that he could release the power he had been using to unite the two. As with most aspects of Nature, the Fire did not want to die before its time. Tay only needed to tap into the Fire's desire to live and to keep it going long enough for the Wind to reach her old ally.

With his job done, he returned to the mouse's body and brought his attention back to the cage that he was in. Now that the Wind had freed the Fire, it was time for him to be freed.

~~~~~~~~~~~~~~~

At the camp entrance of the second path he took, William was finally able to break free of the careening birds and enter the edge of the camp, but instead of yelling the warning that he had intended to yell, he yelled another. "Fire!" he shouted as he watched the flames from several campfires leaping to connect with the material of the nearby tents. In a surreal moment, the flames almost appeared to dance on the wind, leaping from tent to tent as they spread to engulf the entire edge of the camp. After staring in surprise for a moment, William came to life himself, turned, and ran to grab a nearby bucket. He hoped he wasn't too late.

~~~~~~~~~~~~~~~

Razgar smelled the smoke at the exact moment that he heard William's warning cry. He ran from his newly acquired tent as several others ran from theirs and immediately turned their attention to the flames. During the ensuing clamor and chaos, Razgar forgot all about the mouse left behind in the tent. His priority was to see what had caused this new disaster. If the guard had accidentally moved the crystal or forgotten to tie Julia's hands, and she was responsible for this latest conflagration, heads would roll. Razgar wondered why he couldn't find people who were capable of following simple orders. He knew that he deserved at least that much.

Chapter Thirty-Seven

Gern had been about to catch up to William just as he entered the clearing. He watched from the shadows as the camp came to life and dealt, yet again, with fire. Except that this time instead of one fire, there were several fires burning all over the grounds. The wind was whipping the flames into a frenzy, and Gern knew that he could use the chaos to find Taryn and Julia.

As he was contemplating which tent they might be in, he recognized Skye and Reggie circling above him. They were hovering over one tent in particular almost as if they wanted him to notice it. Gern though it was a sorry day when he took advice from birds, but he didn't have any better ideas. Those damn birds were trying to tell him something, and he was sure as hell going to listen. He crept to the rear of the tent they were circling and snuck in; behind him, Skye and Reggie landed and followed.

~~~~~~~~~~~~~~~

Meanwhile Julia was still working with the Wind and now the Fire. She knew the minute they united and wondered why she and Tay had been so oblivious to pairing the two before. We've been shortsighted, she thought to herself. We were only focused on what we saw as the strongest allies for us, never exploring other options. It was a lesson well-learned, and one she wouldn't soon forget.

Now that the Wind and Fire were united and moving on their own, she was also able to connect with Reggie and knew that she and Skye were trying to help Tay. She could hear the guard outside her tent yelling that he would stay with her while the other went to help with the fire. She also heard Razgar approach and quickly fell to the floor on the bedroll hoping that he would believe that she was asleep. She used her body to shield her hands so they would appear to still be tied. The more time that she and Tay had before Razgar caught on, the higher their chance of success.

Taryn saw Gern enter the tent and felt hope and joy enter his heart at the sight of the big man. Skye spotted Taryn immediately, and she and Reggie crossed right over to him, but Gern ignored all of them as he looked around trying to uncover the reason the birds had led him to this tent. It was obviously empty of everything but a mouse. Gern couldn't believe his eyes. The damn fool birds were picking at the lock trying to free the mouse. Was that what this was all about? Dinner?

Taryn squealed in frustration and agitation as he realized that Gern would ignore him in his current state. He started to rage against the bars of the cage. Why hadn't he told Gern of his plan to sneak in early and share the strategy with Julia? Why hadn't he shared more information about his ability to shapeshift with Gern? He knew that he could trust the man. Taryn realized that he had behaved like a greedy child who enjoyed keeping secrets. He hadn't wanted to divulge too much, and now it might be too late.

Gern saw the little mouse struggling to get free. He realized that the creature was probably smelling the fire and panicking as he sensed the flame's approach. Gern knew if he freed the mouse that the Hawk and Rook would eat him. The damn birds were trying to get at him even now. He shooed the birds away and lifted the lock saying, "You pick your death, little one - either someone's meal or fried mouse."

At that moment, chaos erupted all over the British camp as Johann's army attacked. Knowing the cause of the noise, Gern hurried to join his men. At the exact moment that Gern was rushing out of the tent and into the fray, Razgar was rushing into the tent. The ensuing crash between the two men clearly went in Gern's favor, and Razgar was unceremoniously knocked to the ground. The much smaller man was no physical impediment to Gern who barely broke his stride as he stepped over him and hurried off to help his men.

Razgar, who had been entering the tent to spirit away his tiny prisoner, muttered a brief curse and pulled himself off the ground. Neither man had taken much notice of the other as both were focused on a goal of a different nature.

When he brushed off his robes and entered the tent, Razgar was dismayed to find it empty. He overturned pillows and threw belongings about in a futile attempt to uncover the tiny creature. Now the full force of the swearing that Razgar had held back a moment ago erupted from him. But there was no one present to be frightened by his diatribe. For only moments before, the tiny mouse had run out of the back of the tent followed by two birds - one of whom was watching him like a Hawk.

~~~~~~~~~~~~~~~

Julia, who was oblivious to her brother's recent escape, was, however, aware of the chaos outside and knew what must be occurring. For once, she didn't stop to plan or think, but grabbed the silver sword and ran from the tent wielding it like a Valkyrie. The first casualty of this newly impetuous woman was the startled guard who was knocked over the head and left unconscious.

Meanwhile, Taryn had quickly found a quiet corner at the edge of the camp and shapeshifted back to himself. He slipped into a nearby tent and donned some clothes. Now, he had to find Julia and help his men to fight. But before he could do that, he had to find a weapon.

You will have one soon enough. There's a guard running this way. You can knock him out and take his weapon. Hide quickly. He approaches now.

Taryn knew enough not to question Skye but acted at once and hid behind the trees. He caught William off guard and knocked him unconscious with the very branch that Gern had been planning to use earlier. He glanced at the man on the ground, grabbed his sword, muttered a quick apology, and ran back into the fray. Reggie and Skye immediately took to the air and followed. Even as he was running into battle, Taryn was communicating with Skye.

Skye, find Julia and get her out of here.
Reggie will go find her. I'm staying with you.

157

Taryn realized that Reggie would probably leave to seek Julia anyway and that he had a more pressing errand for Skye.

Fine. Reggie can go after my sister. Just keep communicating with each other and me.

As Reggie took off into the air, Taryn mindlinked his next request. *Skye, I need you to go and find Razgar.*

I don't want to leave you.

Please, Skye. Don't argue. We don't have time for this. I need you to be my eyes and ears and follow Razgar. If I stop him, I can change the outcome of this war. Now, go. Find him!

Skye didn't like this latest order one bit, but she knew that Taryn was right. She altered her course with an **As you wish** and went off in search of her prey.

As soon as that was settled, Taryn devoted his full energy to the battle before him. On another side of the camp, Julia was fighting just as hard as her brother. Reggie had found her and was circling above, calling out warnings and advice from her advantageous position.

Although Reggie had found her target successfully, Skye was not having as much luck with hers. Razgar was nowhere to be seen. She widened her grid and flew on.

Chapter Thirty-Eight

On the ground, Taryn and his men were steadily winning the battle. Carlson's men fought well, but the odds were against them. The multiple fires had thrown them into a panic, the winds had crashed down many small trees which in turn had covered equipment, and now they had been attacked when unprepared. And Carlson himself had just discovered that his magical sword was no longer very magical.

Just as it appeared that the battle was winding down and Johann's army would triumph, the tide started turn in Carlson's favor. Both Julia and Taryn felt the energy shift within seconds of its occurring. They knew that the seemingly random happenings were anything but random.

The first drops of heavy rain helped to put the fires out, the next started to flood the swamp and block off possible escape routes for Taryn and his men. Now the Wind, which had earlier partnered with the Fire, found a new teammate. Wind-driven rain was blinding some of Taryn's men, and they were making some fatal moves. Some of his best soldiers were being killed.

Taryn, are you there?

Julia, where are you?

Don't worry about that now. We have to find Razgar and stop him.

I know. But where the hell is he?

Julia heard the warning growl behind her and turned in time to kill the soldier who had been sneaking up on her. She took one look at the Wolf and fled for the nearby tent. There she found what she was looking for.

Wolf, I need you to find this man. Please hurry.

The Wolf sniffed the material and pointed his nose in the air. *Tay, I might have something. The Wolf is here.*

Taryn felt his blood grow cold. *What? She's supposed to be protecting Thomas.*

She wouldn't have come if Thomas weren't safe. We can't worry about that now. We have to find Razgar. Julia was following the Wolf who was now trotting at a steady pace.

159

*Hurry. We're tracking through the eastern part of the camp –
near the trees by the stream. Have Skye lead you to us.*
I'll be there.

As the scent became stronger, the Wolf began to run
more quickly. Julia and Reggie needed no urging to speed up
their pace as well. They were running through the trees when
Taryn and Skye joined them. The two humans and three
creatures raced on, desperate to find Razgar before it was too
late to stop him.

All around them the earth was alive with the storm. Bolts
of lightning and crashes of thunder were creating a spectacle of
light and sound. Animals were scurrying to find cover even as
the group ran on regardless of their own vulnerability.

A bolt of well-timed lightening illuminated Razgar who
was standing on a low hilltop just outside the British camp. It
was a wisely chosen vantage point from which to orchestrate
the storm. When the allies ran into the clearing, the sorcerer's
focus on controlling the elements was so intense and the noise
of the storm so loud that he was barely aware of the arrival of
his enemies.

Razgar hadn't had an opportunity to set up strong
protection around himself because time was short. He had
precious few minutes to turn the tide of this war. If he didn't pay
complete attention to the storm which was building, it would be
too late, and his army would be defeated. In the back of his
mind, he knew that Taryn and Julia would eventually come, but
he didn't count on its being so soon.

Upon finding Razgar, the siblings didn't waste a
moment in discussion. They immediately went into action while
the allies waited nearby, watching for an opportunity to assist in
any way possible. Taryn stood at the edge of the clearing,
focused, and pulled in all of the energy at his command. He
thought of Razgar's attempt to destroy his family and all that he
loved, and he used his anger to overcome his natural fear and
attempt something he would normally never do. Using the
tallest nearby tree and the water as markers, he purposely
placed himself in the most direct path of the lightning. Even as
he was doing this, he knew that the strike would most likely kill

him, but he could see no other way. He was willing to give his life in a desperate attempt to save his family.

As he stood waiting for a force that would be his salvation or his death, he felt a calm come over him. He was so still that he could feel the subtle change in the air as the energy shifted and began to grow. Suddenly, as the energy became as intense as it seemed it could, it was released in a powerful lightning strike. Before he could think about his actions, he threw his body toward the strike and caught a wayward spark from the unpredictable and volatile energy in his hand. He was unaware of the pain searing his palm as he used the lightning's power to form the largest fireball he had ever created. Later, in a more leisurely moment, he was heard to claim that it was the largest fireball **anyone** had ever created.

In the meantime, Julia had circled the hill and climbed up behind the sorcerer who was busy escalating the storm and creating the chaos which would serve his men. When she reached the hilltop, Julia launched herself at Razgar while holding the silver sword aloft and screaming with all of her pent up frustration. The startled sorcerer turned to face his assailant and the angry Wolf who was running beside her and raised his dagger to attack. At the precise moment that he was about to thrust his dagger toward Julia, he was struck from behind by the fireball.

Razgar, who fell to the ground with a potentially mortal wound, was numb to the physical pain as he realized that the pair had bested him. He thought fleetingly that he had done something that he swore that he never would do; he had underestimated his enemy. As he looked up at Julia and her Wolf standing over him, he felt all of the bile towards Johann and his family rise to the surface. How arrogant and smug they all were; they had such belief in their abilities. He had been planning to change all of that. If he hadn't gotten careless at the end, he **would** have changed all of that. Years of careful planning, and he was thwarted just as he was about to triumph. Now the glory was theirs.

Even as he lay dying, Razgar realized that he could never let that be. He had one very dangerous option that he had been trying to avoid, but now he would take it. Ironically, he was doing something very similar to what Taryn had just done. He was risking everything in this moment. He raised his hand to his mouth as he coughed up some blood. He knew he didn't have long now but his hatred was so strong that he was determined to tarnish their victory with his last breath. He struggled to remain conscious long enough to say what he had to say.

While Taryn cooled his burning and blistered palm in the river, Razgar spoke to Julia and used his final words as the only weapon remaining to him. "You may think you have bested me, but you haven't." He paused and winced as a wave of pain washed over him. "Thanks to me, your family line has been broken. I may be gone, but the seeds that I have planted will be sown. Death will come for you, too."

Julia looked with pity at the man who had let hatred twist his life. "Death comes for us all, but for us it will be a long time in coming. With you no longer a threat, we're all safe."

Razgar managed a small smile and said, "You are foolish and naïve if you think that's true. Once again, very predictable."

She arched an eyebrow. "You're right, Razgar. I could have predicted this very ending. I told you not to count us out."

Razgar coughed up some more blood, and his anger flared at her smug demeanor. "And now, that's exactly what you're doing with me. You never learn, do you?"

"You're dying – even you must know that."

"I may be dying, but I go knowing that I have planted seeds of destruction which will soon be reaped. Your brother is mine."

Taryn, who had joined his sister on the small hill and had heard these last few sentences, exchanged a look with Julia. Then he shrugged and said, "I'm right here, Razgar, and I'm fine. You haven't got me, or anyone else for that matter."

Razgar's final sound on earth was a mirthless laugh. He breathed his last as the pair stood in silence for a moment, pondering his final words and all that had come before them. Even though they could make no sense of what Razgar had said, each of them found it unnerving for reasons that they couldn't fully comprehend.

When they realized that they wouldn't make sense of the strange pronouncement, the siblings let it go. They had to. Then they each took a moment to be still and let the truth sink in. This war that they had not started and never wanted was finally over. Each sent out a silent thanks to all of their allies and acknowledged all of the support that they had received.

When they had truly assured themselves that Razgar had breathed his last, the silence was broken, and Julia spoke the question that was on both of their minds. She turned to the Wolf, who was by her side, and asked, *What about Thomas? Is he safe?*

He's safe, Julia. He's hiding in the forest with the fairies and the rest of the wolf pack. I'll take you to him when you're ready.

After Julia shared the Wolf's words, Taryn looked up from where he was crouched beside Razgar and said, "I'm coming with you. I need to see him for myself. But first, I have to check on my men. You can wait here if you want."

Julia shot him a look. "You must be kidding, Tay. After all we've been through, we stick together."

Taryn laughed. "Okay, Jules. I guess we've earned that."

"I should say so. You would have been proud to see me fighting."

"With what?"

"This sword I found." She held it out for him to see.

Taryn looked at the plain silver sword, which he had used earlier for the enchantment, and smiled. "I guess it was just as well that I had to leave that behind when I shapeshifted."

"This **is** the sword then. I had a feeling it might be. But how did you get stuck having to shapeshift?"

"How did you get caught?"

Julia laughed and shrugged. "I guess we have a lot to catch up on."

Taryn threw his arm around his sister and laughed. "C'mon. You can start explaining while we walk back to camp."

Just as the two were heading down the small hilltop, they heard a large crashing noise accompanied by a loud war whoop. They looked over just in time to see Gern dash into the clearing, fully armed for battle.

Taryn chuckled. "Better late than never, Gern."

"Damn you both to hell and back. I had a small war to fight before I could get here." Gern relaxed his military posture and glared at them. "Someone left me in charge and then set out to get himself killed."

"I left the army in the best hands I had other than my own. How did it go back at the front?"

"We had a bit of trouble for awhile, but it's all quiet now. Most of Carlson's remaining soldiers fled or surrendered. We have Carlson himself in a tent ready for you to question."

"What are we waiting for then?"

Gern blushed as he glanced at Julia. "Glad to see you're fine too, Julia."

"Thanks, Gern."

Realizing that now that she was safe, he was mad at her too, Gern added, "Although you're a damn fool too."

Julia burst out laughing at the candor. "Thanks, Gern."

Taryn, who had been watching the brief exchange closely, started to say something but stopped himself when he felt his sister's elbow in his side. Instead, he contented himself with a chuckle. That, however, was squelched by a warning glare from Gern. Finally, he had to settle for whistling a happy little tune as he threw his arms around Julia and Gern. The trio walked through the woods toward camp accompanied by a Wolf, a Rook, and a Hawk. And they wouldn't have had it any other way.

Chapter Thirty-Nine

Several hours later, Taryn was satisfied that everything back at the camp was under control. There had been some losses but not as many as he feared. Most of the British had fled but those who were left were safely under guard. Gern and his other officers had organized details to bury the dead and treat the wounded. Before he took his leave, Taryn spoke with Gern. Satisfied that all was well in hand, he and Julia set off in the early hours of the morning.

By late afternoon they had reached Sarah's, and now the entire group was seated inside the comfortable cottage exchanging stories of the many events that had occurred in the past few days. Between the humans and the animal allies it was a full house, but Sarah wasn't complaining. She was just happy that everyone was alive and well.

After what felt like hours of listening to Thomas recite all of his exciting adventures with the fairies and the wolves, Julia and Taryn finally had a chance to pose the question they had been waiting to ask. It went right to the heart of the matter, and they had exchanged some heated words about it during the ride to Sarah's.

Simply put, Taryn felt that the Wolf should have never left Thomas. The Wolf was silent on the topic and simply said that Thomas would explain everything. Julia was convinced that the Wolf would never have left Thomas unless she knew it was safe to do so. Thomas settled the whole issue once they were able to turn his attention to that part of the story, which was the least exciting part as far as he was concerned.

"But Thomas, how did you know to go into the woods? How did you know where to go so you wouldn't get lost or hurt yourself?" Taryn asked his son.

Thomas shrugged at the simplicity of the question. "The Wolf told me."

Immediately, Julia knew what had happened and realized that in all of the excitement, they had forgotten to tell Tay.

Taryn frowned. "What do you mean she told you? It's not as if she can talk."

Thomas erupted into giggles when the Wolf snorted and made a funny noise. Julia quickly joined in on the laughter as the Wolf projected her thoughts. "Of course she can, Dad. Do you want to know what she said now?"

"No, I do not." Taryn looked indignant as he was sure that it had been about him.

Julia piped in. "We forgot to tell you. We made a really wonderful discovery while you were gone." She paused and watched her brother, wanting to see his reaction to the stunning news. "Thomas can understand what the animals verbalize."

"WHAT???" He looked at each member of the gathered group to see whether they were joking at his expense.

Sarah joined in. "It's true. I saw it myself. Reggie flew back with your note telling us that Julia had been captured. She must have gone to tell the Wolf after she left us. We were all having lunch two days ago when the Wolf scratched at the door to come in. She went right over to Thomas and started making some noise. The next thing I knew Thomas told Nanny and me that he was going with the Wolf to hide in the forest." She looked at Taryn whose disbelief was written all over his face. "He said that Julia wanted him to go."

"And you just let him go? A five-year-old alone in the forest?"

"But Dad, I wasn't alone!" Thomas said in the exasperated tone that only a five-year-old can use.

"It's true, Tay. You saw the protection yourself as we rode up."

When Taryn and Julia were still miles away from the clearing where Thomas was hidden, they saw their first wolf. After that, they spotted several more at different checkpoints along the way. As soon as the wolves recognized Julia's ally, they backed off and let them pass untouched. Most of them then fell in step and accompanied the riders on their remaining journey to pick up Thomas and return to Sarah's. By the time they arrived at the cottage by the pond, they had quite a large wolf pack running beside them. Despite this friendly posse,

166

Julia had no doubt that the wolves would have attacked if anyone had posed a threat to Thomas.

Further proof of the protection surrounding Thomas came as Taryn and Julia neared the fairy bower. The two siblings became lost and disoriented in woods that they knew almost as well as their own backyard. On the third attempt to find the clearing, they realized that the fairies had placed a spell around it and sent one of the wolves to have them release it. Shortly thereafter, they found Thomas sleeping soundly in a small wooded shelter. Standing beside him was the biggest buck that Julia had ever seen.

Taryn finally had to concede that Thomas had been well protected. "Maybe I overreacted. I've had a nerve-wracking few days. I apologize, Wolfie. Can you forgive me?" Taryn absently reached out and tapped the Wolf's head.

The Wolf grumbled and Thomas looked at his father. "She says she's not a dog. She doesn't want you to pet her."

"She lets you and Julia pet her."

Thomas shrugged, wisely deciding that this was one time that he should probably keep quiet.

Taryn looked at his son and asked a question that was still plaguing him. "Thomas, the clearing is a few hours ride from here. Did you walk all that way?"

"No, Dad. I rode."

"A horse?"

"No." Thomas giggled, enjoying the game.

"The Wolf?" The Wolf raised her eyebrows and looked at Julia. She answered this one. "I don't think so."

"I give up." Taryn threw his arms up in exasperation. "Tell me."

"A stag."

"What?"

"Yup. When the Wolf and I went outside there was a huge," Thomas held out his arms as far as they could stretch, "stag waiting for me. Sarah helped me climb on, and the Wolf carried my food and water in a pack. It was a little hard to hold on with my arm, but we went slowly."

Sarah piped up. "It's true, Taryn. I wouldn't have believed it if I hadn't seen it for myself."

"What if it had been a trick, Thomas? What if those animals had been sent to harm you or kidnap you?"

Thomas was clearly exasperated by his father's lack of faith. "Dad, first of all, I know the Wolf, and Julia said she would always care for me because Julia loves me, and the Wolf loves Julia. And second, Tiger said it was okay." Thomas paused and patted his father's hand, "Dad, I'm a big boy. I can take care of myself. Besides, you and Julia still get into trouble, and you're old."

The group laughed, and the earlier tension was eased. Taryn had to admit that Thomas had followed the correct procedure for identifying whether the situation was safe, and he shared that with his son.

"I'm proud of you, Thomas. You've done well."

"I agree." Julia piped in her support as well. "Your father and I couldn't have done better."

Thomas puffed out his chest with pride and said, "Thank you," and then he listened to the noise and said, "The Wolf wants to know if she can leave now. She has some other things to do."

Julia turned to the Wolf and mindlinked.

Thank you, friend. I knew that I could trust you.

You're welcome. The Wolf looked at Julia. Then she turned to Taryn, snorted in a disgusted manner and proudly marched out through the door that Thomas was holding open.

Thomas hesitated, afraid to hurt his father's feelings. "I don't think she likes you, Dad."

"She never has."

Julia piped up. "Her feelings are hurt, Thomas. After all these years, your father didn't trust her." She shot her brother a look.

Taryn shrugged and held his hands up. "Okay, enough already. I apologized. What more does she want?"

Sarah's common sense was evidenced once again. "She's a female, Taryn. It'll take a lot more than one brief apology for her to forgive you."

Taryn groaned, "Great. I probably won't hear the end of this one for years. Julia still remembers things I did when I was ten."

168

"Oh, yes, that reminds me, Thomas. Did I ever tell you about the time your father got stuck up a tree and I had to save him..."

"Hey, two can play that game. Aunt Julia almost blew the castle up mixing one of her potions. It started when she decided that she could..."

~~~~~~~~~~~~~~~~

Thomas learned a lot of very old secrets that evening as the small group continued the light-hearted banter around the dinner table. Sarah and Nanny also had plenty of stories to share from the sibling's youth and were quick to join in with their own tales.

After the dinner was eaten and a heavy-lidded Thomas had gone to bed complaining that he would miss all the fun, Taryn and Julia caught Nanny, Sarah and each other up on the stories they had edited in front of Thomas. That took some time and they were all quite sleepy when the tales had been told. Nanny and Sarah excused themselves for the evening, while Julia and Taryn remained by the hearth.

"You know what still bothers me, Tay?"

"No. What?"

"That last remark that Razgar made about having my brother. Are you sure that you're okay?"

"I'm fine, Julia. No more dizziness."

"How's your arm?"

He held it out for her inspection, moving it around freely to show its easy mobility. "Healing nicely thanks to you and Sarah." He continued on as she inspected the dressing and rewrapped it for the evening. "Stop worrying. Razgar was dying. He probably didn't know what he was saying."

She conceded a bit. "Maybe. But something still doesn't feel right about it."

"You worry too much. That's how this whole thing started, with you worrying that I had been captured. Remember? So stop already."

Julia was still unconvinced, but not quite sure why. "Maybe you're right." She hesitated, knowing there was more to

169

say, but not quite sure what it was. "Well, I guess we should get some sleep."

Taryn smiled at the sister he knew all too well. He knew that no matter what he said, she wouldn't be able to let this go until she had worked it through to some sort of conclusion. "Good idea. Try to do just that." He leaned over and kissed her on the cheek. "Night, Julia."

"Night, Tay."

Chapter Forty

That night Taryn had one of the dreams he referred to as a 'dream of freedom.' He was flying with Skye. The two were enjoying themselves with aerial acrobatics alternating with peaceful drifting on the currents. After a while, Skye disappeared, and Taryn was joined by Julia who was flying as the Rook. For once, she wasn't practicing strategy and war tactics but was also enjoying flying along and relaxing. As the two made lazy sweeping arcs, they noticed another bird flying a short way back. It was a gray dove. She seemed to be following them, wanting to play but not sure how to join in.

Suddenly the mood shifted, and Taryn's dream flashed to a new scene. The dove was now lying on the ground. An arrow had pierced her body, and she trembled in pain. A tall man walked over to her and picked her up none too gently. The man held the skewered dove aloft by the shaft of the arrow and raised his face to the pair flying above. He started to laugh and mock them while shaking the poor dying bird up and down.

Taryn woke with a start. Razgar! The man holding the bird had been Razgar! But Razgar was dead. Why was he showing up in one of Taryn's dreams?

Taryn was so rattled by the dream that he couldn't go back to sleep. He decided his best option was to get out of bed and try to walk it off. He dressed quietly so as not to wake the others and strode into the edge of the forest clearing where he met the Stag. After the two went for a run, he found himself asking for advice about the dream.

I'm worried that the dove was a representation of Thomas.

Why would you think that?

Who else would it be? Father?

As you know, dreams are full of symbols. It could be anyone.

True. But Julia and I both work with winged allies. As Thomas comes into his power, perhaps he will work with a Dove.

Perhaps. Have you seen proof of that?

No, Taryn conceded reluctantly, *I haven't.*

Do you believe that Razgar can still hurt any of you?

I don't know what to believe. I didn't want to alarm Julia, but I also found Razgar's final words a bit unnerving.

Why don't you journey and find out who the dove is?

Maybe I will. I didn't think I needed to worry about this any more, but there's obviously something that is still unfinished.

Perhaps it would be wise to uncover just what that is.

Let's hope I can.

~~~~~~~~~~~~~~~~

It wasn't until much later in the day that Taryn was able to follow up on his conversation with the Stag. He spent most of the day with his son, riding out to visit and thank the fairies and walking through the forest.

Thomas showed him many of the plants that he had studied and explained how to use them. Taryn was impressed with his son's innate ability with the plants, but he was even more impressed with his genius for understanding the creatures around him and what they were saying.

As the sun was lowering in the sky, Taryn decided to take Thomas' instruction even a step further. The two were seated and leaning against an ancient oak tree that was at the edge of the fairy clearing.

"Do you know how you can understand the animals and what they are saying?" Thomas nodded as Taryn continued, "There are others in the forest who would also speak if you listened."

"You mean the fairies?"

"Well, yes, the fairies, but also those who appear not to be living in the same way that we are."

Thomas gave his father a puzzled look. "Who?"

"Thomas, the trees and the rocks have been here a long time - longer than any of us, even Grandfather. They have great wisdom to share if we only listen."

"Really?"

"Really." Taryn hesitated for a moment. "Do you want to try?"

"Okay." He paused. "How?"

Taryn smiled at his earnest young son. "First, we have to become really quiet. Relax your mind like you do right before you fall asleep."

Thomas settled back against the tree and Taryn waited for him to ease himself into a calmer state. "Now as you slowly breathe in and out, try to connect with the spirit of the tree. Sense its presence. Feel your breath go into the tree and the tree's breath come into you." Taryn listened to his young son's steady breathing for a minute or two. "Good. When you feel you have connected with the tree and become aware of its life force, greet it. You can then ask it a question or ask what it might like to share with you."

Several moments passed as the father and son sat quietly side by side. While Thomas was occupied working with the oak, Taryn tried to tap into his dream and uncover the identity of the gray dove. When that didn't work, he journeyed to his teacher and queried him. Although he did receive some clues, he was as frustrated by his teacher's response as Julia had been by Brigid's.

You will have to uncover this mystery for yourself. It is part of your learning. I will, however, help to put your mind at ease and tell you that the dove represents neither Thomas nor your father.

That does help, thank you. Am I correct in sensing the danger to this life?

You are.

But how can Razgar hurt this person if he is dead?

Razgar's power still lives. He has planted a poison which will spread if left unchecked.

Does this person know of the poison?

He does not.

Is there anything else that you can share?

Remember that there are many forms of poison. Some are spread with potions, some are spread with words or deeds.

And Razgar was a master of both.

173

True.

But how can words kill someone?

They can plant seeds of hatred or suspicion that will grow if the ground is fertile enough for them to take root.

That's what happened to Razgar. He spent years hating us, and it grew so much that he wanted us all dead.

When the hatred takes over, one can act in rash and often lethal ways.

I still don't understand what this has to do with me. Can't you tell me more?

I cannot. It would change the course of the future if I did. You must solve this puzzle on your own.

Taryn sighed. *Great. Another mystery to solve.*

Perhaps your sister has some clues that would help you.

Perhaps. Knowing Julia she has been stewing about it all day. I'll ask her after dinner.

~~~~~~~~~~~~~~~

A few minutes later, after Taryn returned from his visit with his teacher, Thomas opened his eyes and smiled at his father. "The tree talks, Dad!" he said, with all of the excitement of a child making a marvelous discovery.

Taryn was delighted by his son's excitement. "I know Thomas. What did he say to you?"

"It's a SHE tree, Dad! She said that she loves the fairies, too, and that she and her family help to keep them safe. When you had trouble finding me yesterday, it was because she was helping to hide us."

"I believe that, Thomas." Taryn nodded at his son. "You did a good job."

"*Did* you have trouble finding me?"

"Only for a while. I will always be able to find you. You're my son."

"Just like you're Grandpa's son."

"Yup. Just like it. Now how about if we go back to Sarah's and get something to eat. We have a long ride home and all of this work has made me hungry."

"Okay, but Dad, if everyone in the forest can talk, you can sure spend a lot of time listening."

"That's true, Thomas. But remember that not everyone who talks has something worthy to say. You will have to discover who is wise for yourself. You will also discover that certain trees or rocks prefer to remain silent, and others will love to talk whenever you can find the time. It's all a matter of practice."

Thomas jumped up and tugged on his father's hand. "Okay, Dad. Let's go. I have to go and see what Sarah's pond has to say."

Taryn laughed at his son's enthusiasm. "Maybe tomorrow and only with Julia or Nanny nearby. I wouldn't want you to fall in."

Thomas' eyes clouded over. "Why can't you come?"

"Thomas I have to go back and rejoin the army. Gern and the men are waiting for me and holding Carlson until I get back."

"But, Dad…"

"With some luck, I won't be too long. Then we can spend a lot of time together."

"Julia, too?"

"Julia, too. But for now I have to go and do my job. Just as you need to do your job and learn all you can from Sarah while you're here."

Thomas sighed and said, "Okay, Dad. I don't want you to go, but I understand."

"I know you do, Son."

~~~~~~~~~~~~~~~~

The two rode back to Sarah's, and on the way, Thomas said hello to almost everything they passed. It was an amused and proud Taryn who returned to the small cottage with his son. Dinner was an even livelier event that evening as everyone was rested and had thought of more stories to share and secrets to tell. Gales of laughter and shouts of "Don't you dare tell that!" echoed off of the four walls.

Later that night when things had calmed down, Taryn shared his dream and his teacher's words with Julia. She was as befuddled as he and couldn't think of any answers to offer. Even by replaying all that had occurred, they couldn't come up with any idea as to the meaning of the dream.

She did have something else to share, however. While Taryn and Thomas had been off all day, Julia had been developing an addition to their firelink powder. She gave the mixture to Tay to pack in his saddlebags.

"This new powder should prevent anyone from eavesdropping on our firelinks. I have enclosed the additional herbs as well as the recipe."

"That's great, Julia. As far as we know, Razgar is the only one who has seen us in the firelink, but I'd rather not take any chances."

"Actually it was that guard, William, who saw us. I forgot to tell you that. Razgar needed him whenever he wanted to intercept our communication." She told her brother about William's discovery of them one evening and subsequent reporting to Razgar.

"Really? That's strange, isn't it? Why would a sentry from the Highlands be able to pick up the firelink?"

"I have no idea. Remember how Father used to try to spy on us and couldn't?"

"Neither could Phaelon. It used to really annoy him that we could relay things back and forth and he couldn't prevent it."

"I know."

"So why William?"

"I have no idea. None at all."

"Another mystery to be solved."

"At least we'll have time, now that the war is all but over and Razgar's dead."

"What a luxury – time. I can't wait."

Chapter Forty-One

Early the next morning, Taryn took his leave of the little group ensconced in Sarah's cottage and rode out to rejoin the army. Shortly after he left, Skye flew up and reported that all was well back at the castle. She had taken a missive to Johann relaying the news about the battle, although not about Julia's abduction or Razgar and his part in the plan. Taryn thought it best to save that until they were all safely together. No need to worry Johann about something which they had already dealt with.

Skye alighted on the front of the saddle and Taryn untied the return message from his father. Johann was riding out to join the army. He should be there shortly. He had sent word via messenger to Lord Royce about the recent battle and awaited his reply. It was fairly certain that Royce would surrender and end the war, especially with his sorcerer no longer alive, but nothing could be done until they had the official proclamation. After he finished reading, Taryn placed the note in his saddlebag and hurried to join his father. He sincerely hoped that Royce would concede defeat. Then the fighting would be over and he could finally return home with his family.

~~~~~~~~~~~~~~~~

Back at the cottage, the usual routine was quickly reestablished after Taryn left. Thomas and Sarah began their lessons after breakfast while Julia and Nanny set about tidying up. After lunch, Thomas requested that he and Julia do some work talking to the pond and the large rock beside it, and Julia and Sarah agreed that was a suitable undertaking.

While Thomas was connecting with the rock, Julia ventured off to find some herbs that she needed to restock her supply kit. When she returned, Thomas was no longer sitting with his back against the sun-drenched rock. Thinking he had returned to Sarah's for a snack, she hurried up the path to the cottage.

When she entered, she woke Sarah and Nanny who had been dozing lightly by the fire. Neither had seen Thomas since he left earlier with her. Telling them not to worry, she strode off in the direction of the woods. Her senses told her that this was not an emergency.

As Julia neared the clearing, she could hear Thomas giggling even before she saw him. Thinking that he had made a new animal friend, she was unpleasantly surprised to hear a man's voice respond to something her nephew had said. In fact, when Julia rounded the final cropping of trees, she stopped in complete and utter shock. The man that her nephew was talking to was the British guard William.

"Get away from him." Julia immediately went into alert and pulled a dagger from her sheath.

Thomas and William looked at her in shock. Thomas stood frozen to the spot while William immediately raised his arms in a peaceful gesture. "Please, Julia. I didn't mean any harm. I don't even know who he is."

"Thomas. Come here."

Thomas whined, "But, Aunt Julia..."

"NOW." Knowing that tone meant business, Thomas scurried to her side. When he was safely there, Julia turned her attention back to the guard. "What are you doing here?"

"I'm going home. This is the way to my farm."

"You expect me to believe that?"

"Julia, the coastal Highlands can be accessed through this forest. The trip is a bit longer but a lot more beautiful. And there's a fairy bower a few hours back that I like to visit." Thomas gasped and looked at his aunt surprised that anyone else knew of the fairies. "I just met Thomas as I was taking a break and giving my horse a drink."

Julia could see the horse slurping water from the stream, but wasn't fully satisfied yet. Their safe hideaway was compromised now unless she did something. She realized that her options were limited, as she didn't have the heart to kill William. He hadn't treated her poorly when she was a prisoner, and he had even gone so far as to admit that he didn't want to fight in the war. It wasn't his fault where he was born or who his mother had befriended.

So she took the only option that was morally acceptable to her. Memory Draught. That still left her with one problem, however, because now, she would have to find a reason to invite him in to Sarah's so that she could slip the potion into his drink.

She would have to continue the conversation until she found her opening. "Are you deserting the army?"

"I'm sure that word will come shortly that we're discharged. I left a bit early, it's true. I have no heart for war. I've told you as much." His forehead creased with concern. "Lately, I've also been worried about my mother. I am anxious to see her and return to our land."

"Razgar is dead." She watched for his reaction. There was none that she could see.

"We heard."

"My brother and I killed him."

"I know, Julia. You did it in self defense. He was going to kill you. I would have done the same."

"I thought you were his friend."

"No one was Razgar's friend. My mother said he was good to her, but I never liked the man."

"What did he do for her?"

"I don't know. She said he gave her a great gift. All I know is that he used me to trap you and your brother with that stupid fire."

The minute William mentioned that, Julia realized that she had more questions about that interception and how it had occurred. "How were you able to do that? Have you been doing that for awhile?"

"No. I've never done it before and I've never seen anyone else in the fire but you two."

"And you didn't know who we were?"

"No. But Razgar did. He knew immediately - as soon as I told him about seeing you."

Julia puzzled out some more of the missing pieces. "Then you must have also been the one who linked and made me believe that my brother was injured."

"Yes." William hung his head. "And I'm sorry for my part in that. I was under orders. Razgar didn't tell me what he was going to do to you."

"But I still don't understand. How did you do it?"

"He just had me wear one of your uniforms, lie down and pretend that I had been beaten. Then he had me establish the link."

"Again, I ask you. How?"

"He threw some powder in the fire and told me that I was to believe I was your brother and ask the fire to show me my sister."

Julia was baffled by this. It didn't make any sense. Someone shouldn't be able to connect with her by pretending to be related to her. There had to be some vital component of the puzzle missing. But something else had just fallen neatly into place. Now, she had the excuse that she needed to ask William to stay.

Julia turned to him and said, "Parts of this story still don't make sense to me William. Perhaps you'd best come up to the cottage with me. We have some things to straighten out."

William nodded lightly. "Of course. I don't know how much I can help, but I'll try. It's the least that I owe you for my part in all of this."

She nodded. "In exchange, we'll give you some food and ale to help you on your ride home."

"You're most gracious, Julia." William said this so kindly and gratefully that Julia felt a twinge of guilt over the fact that she was manipulating him. Just a twinge. In addition to giving him the Draught, she had to admit that she was truly interested in finding out why William had been able to intercept the link when, to her knowledge, no one else ever had.

Thomas chattered excitedly the whole way back to the cottage, happy to have more company to talk to and that his aunt had put her dagger back in its sheath. Julia wasn't paying much attention to him until he said something that made her pause. "At first, I thought you were Father. But I knew he left. And he rides a black horse."

Julia addressed her nephew. "Thomas, that's silly. Why would you think William was your father?"

Thomas looked at Julia not sure why her tone was so strange. "He looks like Dad. Not exactly. But from the back. He's as tall and his hair is almost the same color."

William shrugged as Julia stared at him. Actually Thomas was right. Their build was almost identical, and they had a similar way of holding their bodies. That must be why Razgar had William play the part of her brother. He must have noticed the similarities that Julia had missed. Leave it to Thomas to pick up on something that had eluded her. "Good observation, Thomas. I hadn't noticed, but you're absolutely right."

Thomas beamed at his aunt, satisfied that he had given the correct answer. Sometimes it was hard to figure out what he was supposed to say. Adults could be so confusing. Julia, who was busy contemplating the memories she would place in their guest's mind, was later to remember Thomas' comparison of William and Taryn and wish that she hadn't dismissed it so quickly. She could have saved herself a lot of trouble.

During the meal, William was a model guest in Sarah's cottage. If Sarah thought it odd that they were entertaining a member of the British army, she kept it to herself. She had learned that Julia usually had a reason for her actions and she wasn't about to question her now. When Sarah saw her slip the potion into their guest's drink, part of the riddle was solved. Obviously, Julia did indeed have some sort of plan.

Chapter Forty-Two

Back at camp, Johann, Taryn, and their officers were marking the end of the war with several draughts of ale and a great deal of camaraderie and celebratory noise. Carlson had received word from Lord Royce and had surrendered; his army was disbanded, and the war was officially over. Taryn had released his own men to march home tonight or to leave with the majority who were heading back to Edinburgh tomorrow. Many of the men had decided to journey home together, so tonight there was celebrating. And plenty of it.

A very drunk Gern was seated by the fire beside Johann and Taryn who were also pretty far into their cups. Gern had taken his share of teasing from Taryn, Johann had been advised of the entire tale, and all three were sharing the brotherhood of victory.

After a few convivial hours, Johann asked Taryn to initiate the firelink so that he could say hello to his daughter and grandson. Taryn agreed and went to his tent to get the powders that would help with the link. When he returned, he opened the portal and saw the inside of the small cottage from the vantage point of the hearth. All three men immediately saw William in Sarah's cottage, and all three reacted with varying degrees of shock. Taryn was the first to recover his voice.

"Julia!"

She turned calmly towards the fire. "Oh hello, Taryn. Father! You look well. Hello, Gern."

"What is that British guard doing there?"

"No need to be rude, Taryn. All is well. Thomas met him in the forest this afternoon. He is enjoying a meal and some ale before he rides home." Julia gave her brother a steady look hoping that he would correctly read her subtext.

Taryn frowned. He knew that Julia was telling him that she had things under control, but he didn't like the situation one bit. "I hope he knows that the war has officially ended, and we are no longer enemies."

William chimed in, "I'm happy to hear that, Taryn, and to be honest, we never were enemies."

He grudgingly agreed, "All right." Then Taryn added, "Julia, Father wanted to see you and Thomas."

"Grandpa!" Thomas, who had left the room earlier to fetch his notebook to show William, had just returned.

Johann, still awkward with this form of communication, leaned toward the flame. "Hello, Thomas, I've missed you."

"I've missed you too, Grandfather. I've learned a lot, though."

For the next ten minutes or so, Thomas spoke with his grandfather while the others listened and added their bits and pieces to his tale. At the end of the firelink, Taryn felt a bit calmer having learned that William was soon to be on his way. When the link was once again closed, he turned to his father who had a puzzled look on his face.

"Father, what is it?"

"This is odd, but there is something nagging me about that young guard."

"What do you mean?"

"I can't quite put my finger on it, but I almost feel as if I've met him."

Taryn remembered his own nagging feelings about William. "Funny, I had the same feeling myself, but it's impossible. He's from the Highlands. When would we have met him?"

Johann, who realized that he had drunk entirely too much ale, gave up struggling with something so trivial and turned back to the party at hand. "It must be the celebration. Tonight, I feel as if everyone is my friend."

To which a very drunken Gern added, "Aye, and there's at least one duplicate of each of them!"

Chapter Forty-Three

After dinner, Julia walked William to the stables and said goodbye. As she mindlinked with him, she erased all memories of the cottage and of his seeing them. Just for safety, she once again had Reggie follow him for a short distance to make sure that he was indeed heading north toward the Highlands and not staking out the cottage or heading back to the British camp to give away their location. A few hours later, the Rook returned to report. Julia was waiting up by the hearth with the window open when Reggie alighted on the sill.

What news, Reggie?

He is indeed heading for the northern coastline.

All is well then. Thank you.

Is he the guard who saw you in the fire?

He is. Why?

He may have more power than he knows.

Why do you say that?

He has a winged ally too.

Julia was surprised by this information. *He does?*

Yes.

She gave the Rook a wry smile. *Not a sparrow, I hope.*

No. A dove. A gray dove.

Julia's heart started to pound in her chest. *Are you sure?*

Absolutely. She followed him into the woods when he arrived and waited outside while William dined with you. She joined him again as soon as he left the cottage.

Reggie, this could be the same gray dove that Taryn saw in his dream!

What dream? You haven't mentioned it before.

Julia proceeded to fill Reggie in on Taryn's dream. After some discussion, they both decided it was worth mentioning to Taryn. That proved to be easier said than done, as getting through to Taryn became something of a challenge. The men had continued the drinking long after the firelink had been closed, and Taryn was in a very deep ale-induced sleep. Julia couldn't rouse him no matter what she did. It would have to wait for morning. She did, however, send Reggie to see if she could find William and track him to his home. She didn't know why, but she felt it was important that they know where he lived.

~~~~~~~~~~~~~~~~

That night Taryn had another dream. In it, he and Julia were working on something that they were brewing over the hearth. It was some sort of a protective potion. From Taryn's vantage point as the dreamer, he could see their backs with their heads bent together over the hearth as they sprinkled herbs into the pot. The siblings stirred the potion that was brewing for a minute and then he saw himself turn to get a new herb on the table. Taryn was startled when he realized that it wasn't he who was working with Julia. It was William.

What was William doing in his place working beside Julia?

~~~~~~~~~~~~~~~~

It was dawn the next morning when a very headache-weary group of men broke camp and prepared to leave for home. As Taryn was packing his belongings, he thought back on his dream and realized it was most likely triggered by the appearance of William at Sarah's. It was fairly easy to explain. He would normally be the one at Sarah's – not William - and that was why he and William had been switched in the dream. Interestingly enough, William was also on his father's mind as he mentioned him later that morning.

"There is something about that young man that nags at me even now."

"You were probably just annoyed that he was there with Thomas and Julia."

"No, I think it was more than that. He seemed familiar somehow."

"He's Scottish, Father. You always think all Scots are part of your family."

Johann chuckled. "Maybe you're right. And speaking of family, have you checked with your sister to make sure that all is well?"

"Not yet. I was going to check when we stopped for a break a bit later. She can always reach me if she needs me. I don't want to wake them; it's still early."

Johann nodded his agreement.

~~~~~~~~~~~~~~~

Later that morning, as they got closer to home, Taryn felt Julia trying to mindlink with him. He told his father and Gern that he was going to stop for a while and find a quiet spot in order to concentrate. As he pulled off to the side of the path, he could feel her urgency, but they were still too distant to connect. He hated to take the time, but he would have to build a small fire. When the fire was burning steadily, he threw the powder in and opened the link. Julia was waiting impatiently by the hearth, and as soon as she shared her news, he understood her excitement.

"But, Julia, we still don't know what this means."

"Obviously Razgar is going to kill William."

"Razgar is dead."

Julia groaned in frustration. "I know that, Tay. But he could have set something into motion before we killed him."

"True. But why show me?"

"I have no idea. Maybe we're meant to stop it."

"I can't just leave everything and ride off to help a British soldier - even if he seems a good enough sort."

"I know. But there has to be something here that we're missing. Your dreams almost always contain clues that we're meant to follow. Have you checked with your teacher?"

"Yes. He says it's for us to figure out. He can't help."

"Great. The last time a teacher said that, it was Brigid, and you remember the mess we ended up in that time."

"Yeah. Let's not do that again." He paused and then added, "I say we ignore it."

Julia looked doubtful. "If you're sure."

"I'm sure. Listen, I'll be there tomorrow to bring you and Thomas home. We can discuss it then if it's still bothering you."

"All right," she reluctantly agreed, "we'll see you tomorrow."

~~~~~~~~~~~~~~~~

Ignoring it proved easier said than done. The two dreams kept replaying in Taryn's mind as he rode back to the castle with his men. Julia also found herself pondering the situation as she went about her work at Sarah's.

It turned out that Johann was to provide the clue that finally shed some light on the situation. He was riding beside Taryn and talking of times past as the two rode back to the castle. Since he had shared the full story of his wife's death, it was as if a dam had opened up, and now Johann wanted to convey more of the life that he and his wife had shared.

He realized that his children knew precious little of their mother, the woman he had loved so deeply. In attempting to quell his own grief, he had not spoken of her and, consequently, had deprived the children of a full sense of their mother and their history. On the ride home, he started to rectify that with Taryn.

He told him all sorts of little, funny, endearing stories about Louisa. Everything he saw on the trip home reminded Johann of another story to share. When Skye flew over and landed on Taryn's arm, Johann recalled his wife's love of the creatures in the kingdom.

"Your mother also loved the winged ones as do you and your sister. I'm sure that you get that connection from her."

Taryn looked at his father in surprise. "Was she an enchanter?"

"Not that I know. Why do you ask?"

"These abilities tend to run in families and I've always wondered where Julia and I got ours from."

"Well it certainly wasn't my family." Johann smiled ruefully. "If I'd had any ability at all, I would have seen this mess coming and prevented it."

"Please, Father," Taryn pleaded, "if we're going to lay blame on that score, then Julia and I deserve a large portion of it."

"Nonsense Taryn, if it weren't for you two we'd all be in a lot worse shape than we are. You get the credit for resolving this situation…and my eternal gratitude as well."

187

"We're fortunate to have powerful allies to aid us."

"Yes, you are, Son."

The two men rode in companionable silence for several minutes. Johann was lost in thoughts of Louisa, while Taryn was thinking of the young woman he was hoping to see in the next few hours.

Skye, can you fly ahead to the castle and find Shira?

Do you want to send a note?

I don't think that's necessary. If she sees you at her house, she'll know I'm not far behind.

True. We've used that as a signal in the past.

I think I'll spend the night with her and then ride out to Sarah's in the morning.

Very well. I'll return after I find her.

Thank you.

Johann and Taryn both watched as Skye took flight. Seeing her reminded Johann of the story he had been about to tell.

"I was going to tell you earlier that your mother used to keep a pet bird in the castle. Her name was Sophie."

Taryn smiled at his father's memory, picturing a tiny finch or sparrow.

"That must be why you were always telling Julia and me to keep our 'damn birds' outside."

"It's true. I wasn't going to put up with that nonsense again." Johann smiled as he recalled the chaos that the bird had caused. "I hated the darn thing. It was always flying about and scattering my papers. I think it knew that I hated it and purposely made a mess of my belongings."

Taryn laughed and said, "Yes. I can imagine Skye doing that to someone she wanted to annoy. What I can't imagine is why you put up with that."

"Because I loved your mother and where she went, so went the dove."

Taryn looked at his father. "It was a dove?"

"Yes. A gray dove."

Suddenly, it all began to fall into place. Now Taryn knew what the dreams had been telling him. He quickly called Skye back to him before she was out of reach. They had to get to Julia.

Chapter Forty-Four

Later that afternoon, the Rook returned and landed by Julia who was walking around the pond.

I'm sorry, Julia. I was unable to locate either William or the Dove.

That's okay, Reggie. Taryn didn't feel that we should follow up on this anyway. I disagree, but I'll wait until he comes tomorrow to talk about it again with him. I'm not going off alone without preparing this time."

That seems wise.

Perhaps I have learned from my past mistakes. At least, I'd like to think so.

Just then the Wolf trotted up to them. **Julia.**

Yes?

Your brother approaches quickly from the south.

What? They were heading for home this morning. What could have happened?

I don't know, but he's riding as if on fire, and Skye is flying above.

It's too bad that Sarah and Thomas are off gathering herbs now. Thomas will be so disappointed if Tay leaves before they return. Hopefully he can stay for a while.

I wouldn't count on it. They seem to be in a hurry.

I guess we'll soon find out why. Come. Let's go up to the cottage and wait for them.

~~~~~~~~~~~~~~~

A short while later, Julia could see the dust from the horse as her brother approached.

"Julia, get your horse. We have to ride NOW."

"Taryn, what is it? Are we in danger?"

"Not us. William."

She looked at her brother, perplexed by his complete change in attitude and the urgency of his tone. "Why is this suddenly so important? You told me to calm down about it."

"I don't have time to explain, but William is our brother."

190

"What?" She stared at him in shock. Her face drained of color as some of the unexplained pieces in the puzzle began to fall into place.

"It's true, Julia. He must be. Don't you see? It's the perfect revenge. Razgar took our brother and had him raised by someone else. Then he enlisted him in the army that fought against us, effectively making us his enemy. And now, he'll have him killed if we don't stop it."

Julia's head was still spinning from all of the information that Taryn had just poured out. "But how could it be? Our brother died with Mother."

"I don't know. I've only just begun to unravel this convoluted mess. We'll see what else we can figure out as we travel. Which way did he head?"

"Northwest for the Highland shore."

"Then let's go."

"Go get my horse while I tell Nanny where we're going and get my saddle bags." She hesitated for only a moment and looked at her brother. "Oh Tay, I hope we're not too late."

Chapter Forty-Five

William arrived home tired but relieved to be there. He wasn't aware of it, but the Memory Draught had been effective. All he remembered was riding straight through the forest and camping out for a night by its edge.

As he dismounted, he was not surprised by how quiet the area was. He and his mother had a small but fertile area of land on the coast. The nearest neighbors were just under an hour away.

He took his horse to the stables, rubbed him down, and fed him. He wondered what his mother might be doing that she hadn't heard him arrive, although he knew that her hearing wasn't what it used to be. In fact, during the last few years he had noticed that she was slowing down, and he had tried to carry even more than his usual share of the farm work.

William often wished that he had siblings, not only to share the workload but for companionship. His mother, who had been older when he had arrived, said that she was happy just to have him. She had been a loving and kind mother, and for that he was grateful; still, it had been a lonely childhood with no siblings or close neighbors.

As William approached the cottage, he noticed nothing amiss. He entered the small home and called out to his mother. When she didn't answer him, the first twinges of anxiety nibbled at the corners of his mind. He found her on her bed and went to gently wake her. Receiving no response from her, he rolled her over. That was when he discovered the dagger partially embedded in her side. William cried out in confusion and shock and pulled the dagger from his mother, throwing it to the floor. He heard her moan and realized that she still lived.

"Mother. Mother." William gently tapped her cheek and tried to rouse her. He felt her forehead and realized that her brow was feverish. As quickly as he could, he undid her bodice and surveyed the damage. The wound was nasty, but if he cleaned it immediately, he might be able to save her.

Because William and his mother lived so far from others, they had to be able to take care of themselves. Both of them had some rudimentary skills with healing herbs and poultices which William employed now. He immediately stanched the blood flow, cleaned his mother's wound and dressed it with the appropriate salves and bandages. Then he put her in a warm nightgown and carried her to the small living room where he settled her to rest on a daybed. Knowing that he needed to keep her warm, he built a fire in the hearth, covered her with a quilt, and pulled up a chair to watch over her.

~~~~~~~~~~~~~~~

Julia and Taryn rode through the night. They reached the northern territory just as the sun was rising. During the long night, Taryn explained how he had pieced the clues together.

"Something about the dreams kept nagging me. I just couldn't let it go."

"I know. I had the same problem, but how did you finally piece it together?"

"As soon as Father mentioned Mother's dove, it all fell into place."

"Did you tell Father?"

"I had to, Julia. He had a right to know."

"I know. I just don't want his heart to be broken if we're too late to save William from whatever Razgar planned."

"I thought of that too. I convinced him that it would be faster if you and I rode out alone. At least that way, we'll be the first to deal with whatever awaits us."

"When will he join us?"

"He agreed to see the men safely settled back in Edinburgh. He'll come shortly after that."

"What if we're too late?"

Taryn looked over at his sister. "We can't be too late, Julia. We have to get there in time."

Chapter Forty-Six

While they had ridden through the night, Julia and Taryn had also discussed several possible ways of locating William's home. They knew it was a coastal farm from his conversation with Julia, but that still left too much ground for them to cover. As they gave the horses a rest and some water, they put the first part of their plan into action. Taryn called to Skye and asked for her help.

Skye, how did you and Reggie first discover that you could communicate with each other?

I don't remember. It seems we always spoke. Just as you and Julia speak in your minds.

But you can't speak to all of the other creatures, can you?

No. Just those of my kind or with whom I have a friendship. You have to work to connect on this level.

But if you two can communicate because of the bond between Julia and me, isn't it possible that you could communicate with the Dove because William is our brother?

It's possible. We can try.

Please do, Skye.

We will need to be close to her.

I know. What if you fly along the coastline as you attempt to reach her?

And if we connect?

Please explain everything that's happened, especially Razgar's threat. Ask her to meet us and bring us to William.

It may be difficult to convince her to trust us.

I know Skye, but we have to try. Julia and I will attempt to reach William while you're working on the Dove.

We'll report back as soon as we can.

~~~~~~~~~~~~~~~

While Taryn had been speaking with Skye, Julia had been busy building a campfire. She wanted to attempt to reach William through the firelink. They had to hope that William currently had a fire burning in his hearth at home, but that seemed a distinct possibility as the late fall mornings in the Highlands were quite chilly.

Taryn and Julia knew that William had seen them in the link before without a conscious attempt to do so on either side. The siblings thought that meant that it might be possible for them to get through if they both focused on it. Of course, there was also a great deal of reliance on coincidence here. William would not only need to have built a fire, but he would also have to be near it when Julia and Taryn tried to link.

~~~~~~~~~~~~~~~

Back in his home, William studied the dagger he had pulled from his mother's side and realized that he recognized the blue and green crest on it. It was the same crest that had been on the dagger that the guards took from Julia when they captured her. In fact, had he been a betting man, William would wager that he was currently holding Julia's dagger in his hands.

William was sick with sorrow and anger. What would Julia gain by wounding his mother? Was this Julia and Taryn's revenge for his playing a part in their capture? Maybe he had misjudged them and Razgar had been right about them all along. They were arrogant, manipulative, and evil; they just kept it hidden better than others.

With the overwhelming combination of grief and exhaustion, William couldn't reason clearly enough to figure things out, nor did he care to try. His only priority now was his mother. He had to get her to eat something. She would need all of her strength to fight off this fever and infection.

He began to prepare some simple broth. It seemed a good place to start. Once it was ready, he tried to get her to sip a bit of it. Gently, he lifted her head and held her in his arms while carefully bringing the cup to her mouth. She moaned and, for a moment, seemed to stir. He couldn't get her to sip the broth, but he thought he heard her mumble his name. When he tried to get her to speak again, she didn't respond. Soon after, she slipped back into a deep slumber. William felt her forehead and realized that she was burning up. He had already done everything he knew to reduce the fever. He couldn't think of anything else other than to keep applying more cold compresses to her head.

Finally he made her as comfortable as he could and resumed his seat by the fire. From there he would be close by and ready to respond to her needs at a moment's notice. William's intention to stand vigil was quickly thwarted. Once seated, his exhaustion caught up with him, and he fell into a light, but troubled, sleep. He was awakened by what he thought was his mother calling his name.

"William. William. Wake up."

"What?" He was groggy from sleep and it took him a few minutes to remember where he was and what had happened.

"William, it's Julia and Taryn." The siblings had decided to let Julia take the lead as she was more familiar to William.

William looked into their faces wavering in the flames and exploded with anger. "How dare you!"

"William, I'm sorry to intrude, but you're in danger."

"What is this? Are you mocking me?"

Julia was confused. "What do you mean?"

"The danger has already been here, and you damn well know it. Thanks to you, my mother is lying here fighting for her life."

Julia gasped. "Who did this?"

"I should be asking you that question. Do you recognize this dagger, Julia?" He held the dagger with the blue and green crest up to the fire. "I believe it's yours."

"I don't know why my dagger is there." She thought back quickly. "I never got it back from Razgar. You know he took it."

"The only thing that I know right now is that someone I love is lying here and may be dying because of this dagger."

Taryn spoke up and tried to reason with the younger man. "Please, William. Think about it. Why would we harm your mother and then contact you? We're trying to warn you that Razgar threatened you."

William couldn't believe what he was hearing. "Why would Razgar threaten me? I told you that he helped my mother and me. And have you forgotten that Razgar is dead?" William shook his head. "You're making no sense."

Julia responded, "Think about it. You just had dinner with me and left Sarah's cottage. How could I have beaten you home? I don't even know where you live."

William was outraged by Julia's blatant lie. "I've never eaten with you. I don't know anyone named Sarah. And if you are as good at enchanting as Razgar claimed, I'm sure that you could have found my home and arrived before me."

Taryn piped in. "We aren't gods, William, and we really are trying to help."

"You've done enough already." He threw the dagger down on the kitchen table. "Leave me alone."

Taryn insisted. "We have to come and talk to you."

Julia tried again. "I can help your mother if you'll let me. I promise."

"I'm not letting you near my mother. You've done enough damage already."

"William, at least put the dagger in the fire so that I can see if there was poison on the end of it. I can tell you which antidote to use. You can trust me to do that at least, can't you? We can do it all through the firelink."

"Go away, Julia, and take your brother with you. I never want to see your faces again." His eyes shone with the anger he felt and the tears that were waiting to be shed. "And if I do, I can promise you that it won't go well for either of you."

With that, William turned his back to the fire and proceeded to his mother's bedside. Realizing that any more communication was futile, Taryn broke the link and turned to Julia. She was the first to speak.

"Damn that Memory Draught. He doesn't remember being at Sarah's."

Trying to lighten the tension, Taryn remarked, "I always said you were a genius at potions."

She groaned. "Oh no, Tay. What are we going to do?"

"I'm more worried about what William could do."

"What do you mean?"

He hesitated, not really wanting to go down that path. "You realize what will probably happen, don't you?"

"Yes. William will hate us for the rest of his life."

"And it will be a very short life." Taryn sat by the fire and motioned for Julia to sit as well. Once she was beside him, he continued. "Think about it, Jules. I would bet that there was poison on that dagger. We know from my experience that it's a method which Razgar favored. But, thanks to you, I had an antidote. William's mother, however, doesn't, which means that she will most likely die. When that happens, he'll be overwhelmed by grief and anger. He won't be thinking clearly, and he'll come after us. And then we'll be forced to kill him." He paused, then added quietly, "I won't let anyone endanger you, or Father, or Thomas - not even my own brother."

Julia felt the tears start to form in her eyes. She understood exactly what Taryn was saying and all of the ramifications. "And then Razgar will win. The family will kill its own." She looked at Taryn and said forlornly. "He was right, Tay; even though he's dead, he does have my brother."

Chapter Forty-Seven

Julia and Taryn sat immobilized for several moments as they tried to figure out a way to find William's home. When Skye and Reggie returned, they also reported a lack of success in their mission. The gray Dove would not even acknowledge them.

Skye reported first. **I don't know if she even can communicate with us. After all, she and William are untrained.**

I know, Skye, but there must be a natural ability present.

Reggie piped in. **I think she heard us. She stayed on the tree branch while we told her the story.**

True.

But she just ignored us. She didn't want to believe what we were telling her.

What makes you say that, Reggie?

I saw her glance at us at different times as we told our tale.

It's true. At one point, I almost thought she would speak, but then she suddenly flew away.

Obviously, she didn't trust us.

Julia sighed. *Why would she? To her, we're the enemy.*

Why didn't you follow her to see where she went? Taryn asked.

We did, but she knew that we were there.

She just flew into the forest and landed. It was clear that she wasn't going home with us watching, so we came back to report to you.

I'm sorry, Julia.

Don't worry. At least you tried. It was a long shot anyway.

Perhaps the Dove will share the tale that we told her with William.

Taryn replied, *I don't think they can communicate with each other yet. I'm not even sure he knows of her. If they were already linked, we would've seen more evidence of it.*

That's true Tay, but there must be some instinct for the work. William could see us in the link without even trying.

Yes, but we were trying to reach him.

Not the first few times. Julia paused, and then added. *We have to figure out how it happened. Let's retrace. We'll go over everything that we did to start the link those times that he might have seen us. Maybe there's a clue there.*

Taryn groaned. *I don't see how that will help. It's just a waste of time.*

Do you have a better idea?

Taryn shook his head sullenly and answered out loud. "No."

Skye piped up. **Reggie and I will fly out and see if we can pick up the Dove's trail. Since she saw us leave, she might have let down her guard and flown home now. We could spot her along the coast.**

If we find her, we'll let you know.

Fine. Thank you both. Julia spoke for the both of them, and then turned to her brother. "Okay, then. What do you do when initiating a link?"

Taryn answered sullenly. "You know that, Julia. This is a waste of time."

"Humor me, Tay. Walk me through it."

"All right. If I have the powders handy, which I usually do, I sprinkle them into the fire and state my intention."

"What do you say?"

"I greet the spirit of the fire and the firelink, and I request their aid in linking with you wherever you may be. The next thing I know, there you are, unless you aren't near a fire or have it blocked. Then I just see a wavering of the flames and a small puff of smoke."

"Right. That's what I do too."

Taryn let his frustration with the situation show. "That accomplished a lot."

Julia bristled at his tone. "You know, Tay, what would help was if you had a suggestion, too. Rather than just putting my ideas down."

"Well, even you have to admit that it was a waste of time."

200

As she prepared to leave, Julia tried to contact Tay and discovered that he had blocked the mindlink. She wasn't worried; she knew that he would lift the block as soon as he calmed down. Right now, she would concentrate on finding her other brother and helping him and the woman he knew as his mother.

After everything was packed up, Julia calmed her mind and went into a journey state. She set her intention for a middle world journey which was a journey that took place in this reality. She asked to be taken to her brother William's house.

When her journey began, she found herself standing on a promontory by the ocean. She scanned out over the water for a few moments and then turned back to see a small farm behind her. Julia looked around for any markers she could find. Places and objects didn't always appear in alternate realities exactly as they did in ordinary reality, so Julia tried to find as many landmarks as she could. The shape of the coast, farms, even large hills and rocks - all could help to locate a person or place. When Julia had perused the area as much as she could from the ground, she shapeshifted into a Rook and viewed it from above. When she was satisfied that she had gleaned all that she might, she flew back to where her body was now, thus creating an aerial map of sorts for herself to follow.

Once Julia had fully returned to her resting body, she contacted Reggie who was already flying back to her. She needed to get a message through to her brother, and she hadn't yet realized that he had lifted the block on the mindlink. As it happened, Taryn had also calmed down and realized that both he and Julia had acted out of tension and frustration. They had each been through a lot in the past few days, and the anxiety had finally escaped. They had blown up with each other simply because they could.

Feeling bad about leaving his sister behind, Taryn had turned around and was riding back to her. He had been riding about twenty minutes when Julia rode in from the opposite direction. She told him about the information that she had retrieved as the two turned toward the coast together. The disagreement had blown over as quickly as they usually did and was completely forgotten as the siblings tried to locate their brother. Skye and Reggie immediately set off to fly ahead and scout for the cottage which Julia had described. They all knew that time saved now could mean the difference between life and death for William's adopted mother.

Chapter Forty-Eight

Back in the cottage, William had taken a short rest and then tried to get his mother to drink some broth again. She seemed to be getting worse and he had no idea why. Perhaps there had been poison on the dagger after all. Finally, she stirred.

"William."

"Mother, I'm here." He ran a cool cloth over her forehead.

"Army. Man."

"I know mother. Johann's man."

"No. Royce."

This was too much for William to process. "What? Are you saying that it was one of our men who did this to you?"

She nodded weakly.

This made even less sense to William than his belief that Julia and Taryn had been seeking revenge. The question he asked next was to himself as much as it was to his mother. "Why?"

Unfortunately, William's mother Marion was not able to answer that question. In retrospect, he realized that she might not have been able to answer it even if she had remained conscious. William hovered by her side and watched helplessly as she became weaker with each passing hour. Nothing he tried did any good; she was slipping away from him.

When Julia and Taryn found the small farm a few hours later, it was almost too late for William's mother. He was seated by her side weeping tears of frustration and didn't hear them arrive.

Julia hesitated in the doorway. She spoke softly, trying not to startle him. "William, we're here. Let us help you."

"It's too late, Julia."

Julia tentatively stepped forward. "Let me see, please."

William stepped back and motioned her over to his mother in the bed. Julia took her cue from him and stepped close to where Marion lay.

Taryn, who was watching William closely for signs of aggression towards them, was relieved that he didn't see any. Before the situation could deteriorate, he spoke. "We had nothing to do with this William."

He looked at them and nodded. "I know. My mother told me."

"Tay, find out what's on this dagger. We don't have any time to waste."

Taryn immediately took the dagger to the hearth. When he held the tip of the dagger in the flames, a small puff of energy was released, and he was able to uncover the poison that had been used. It was the same poison that had been used on him. Luckily, he still had some of Julia's antidote left and raced out to get it from his saddlebags. Meanwhile, Julia had taken her traveling medicine pouch out and had found some potions that would give Marion strength in her battle to fight the poison. William watched helplessly but hopefully as the two siblings worked together to save his mother.

Within a short time, Julia had administered the antidote and the other potions. Now all they could do was wait and watch and make Marion comfortable. While the trio sat vigil, Julia and Taryn shared the story of Razgar and his hatred for their family. As part of the story, they told of William's abduction and everything they knew about what had happened to him as a baby. Even though they tried to tell the story as gently as they could, it was even more shocking to William than it had been to any of them. It made him feel as if his whole life had been a lie and shook its very foundation. Despite the fact that this tale cast doubt on many aspects of his life, there was one thing of which he was absolutely certain.

"My mother is a good woman. She would have never taken someone else's baby," he adamantly stated.

Taryn, knowing that this was not the time to denigrate Marion, hid his own doubts and said, "William, no one is blaming your mother. I doubt she even knew where you came from. Razgar probably told her a lie, and she believed that you were an orphan."

Julia added gently, "Hopefully we can find out more of the story when she wakes up."

"I hope so too, but there's one thing I know for sure. My mother never would have knowingly been part of what Razgar did to you and your family."

Perhaps it was too soon, but Julia said, "You're part of our family too."

William's defenses were up. It wasn't surprising in light of the emotional turmoil of the past several hours. "Don't ask me to disown the woman who raised me and who loved me."

Taryn's tone was conciliatory. "We would never do that, William. And we know that this will take time. We're just asking you to allow us to be part of your life. Let's start there. All right?"

The tension that had been in William's voice earlier was eased a bit by Taryn's tone and words. "All right." He paused and stared at both of them. "But I won't have a bad word spoken about my mother."

Taryn and Julia glanced at each other. They each had their own doubts about Marion and the part she had played in the story, but that wasn't important now. What was important was that William feel their love and acceptance.

Julia said, "I think we can all agree that you love Marion and that she's been good to you. You won't hear any of us ever speak against her."

William looked for assurances. They both nodded and Taryn added, "We promise."

That simple promise alleviated much of the tension that William had been feeling and he responded firmly but gently. "All right then. If we can agree to that, we've got a start. The rest will just take time."

Julia put her hand on his arm. "We know that William. There's no pressure from us. We just want to be here for you."

His eyes started to well up as he looked over at his mother lying on the makeshift bed. He could be losing the woman who was the only family he had known. Taryn and Julia weren't his family; Marion was.

And yet, in some ways having them here made William feel a little bit less alone right now. "Thank you. I'm grateful for the care that you're giving my mother."

207

~~~~~~~~~~~~~~~~

It was a few watchful nights and days that the small group spent together. It gave them time to get to know each other and a chance to unite over a common goal: the care of the woman who was Mother to William. Because Taryn and Julia had lost their own mother when young, they understood the fear in William's heart and did everything they could to ease his worries.

To pass the time while they were waiting and watching Marion and to occupy William's mind, Julia and Taryn shared some tales from their childhood. This sharing of stories was awkward and unsure at the start, but as time marched on, the tales flowed more easily. After a while, they were able to coax William into sharing his stories of growing up in the Highlands. As often occurs with storytelling, moments of laughter and ease arose during the telling and the listening. Whether they were due to the giddiness of exhaustion or the humor of the tale, no one was quite sure. Ultimately, it didn't matter, and the three siblings began to have a sense of each other, much as newly found friends do.

It was into this atmosphere of extremes - laughter, worry and exhaustion - that Johann arrived on the morning of the third day. Skye had met him at Sarah's and guided him the rest of the way. Johann knew that he was arriving at an inopportune moment in his youngest child's life, but he was determined that he would not be kept from his son any longer. He had lost eighteen years thanks to Razgar; he wasn't going to lose another moment.

The reunion of father and son was awkward, and William was even more overwhelmed by the new arrival. It was a difficult enough situation for everyone else present to comprehend and assimilate, but they had the familiarity of each other and the ease that is born of spending years together. Also, they weren't worried about the well being of someone they loved. Thankfully, Johann was aware of the situation and did his best to let his children lead the way. He didn't mind staying in the background; he was just grateful that he was with his children and could support them. He was pleased to see that even though William was a bit unsure with Julia and Taryn and they were still very careful with him, there was a certain bond which had developed over the few days they had spent in each other's company. Johann could see the care and compassion that Taryn and Julia gave to William's mother. He was proud of them for that, and once again, he realized how special his children were. He knew in his heart that William was just as fine a person.

Unfortunately, the lavish care and compassion weren't enough to save Marion. She fought hard but finally succumbed to the poison that had been in her system too long. She never regained consciousness again and was never able to share her part in the winding tale that had been unfolding. Her death left many unanswered questions for all of them. They wondered who the baby was that had been buried with Louisa and why Razgar had chosen Marion to raise William. But discussing those questions inevitably led to doubts about Marion's role in all of this, and William refused to believe ill of his mother. Johann, Taryn, and Julia respected that and, with some difficulty, let it be. They would have time together later to theorize, but for now, the discussion was put to rest along with Marion.

Chapter Forty-Nine

The burial was a simple affair with Marion being laid to rest in a family plot by the ocean's edge. Only the four newly united family members and a few of the less distant neighbors were in attendance. After the prayers had been said, there was a simple spread laid out for the mourners which Julia prepared and presided over. William was grateful for her help; he didn't think that he could have managed alone. When the guests departed, the men went out to take care of the animals for the evening. Doing the regular chores was comforting for William, and the others were only too happy to pitch in. It was a weary group that finally said their good nights and laid down to rest.

The next morning, Johann, Taryn, and Julia knew that the time had come for them to leave. They all had duties to get back to and loved ones whom they missed. No matter how hard Johann tried to convince him, William refused to return to the castle with them. He did, however, finally agree to meet them all at Sarah's in the spring. In addition, Julia was leaving him with the powders and instructions on how to firelink so they could stay in touch with each other.

It was a sad trio that took their leave. As Julia gave William a tentative but loving hug, she said, "Now we'll expect to see you at Sarah's after the planting."

Taryn piped in, "I'm sure that Thomas will be excited to see you again, as well."

William smiled shyly at them. "I promise. I'll be there. Tell Thomas that I'm looking forward to seeing him, too."

Julia added, "And we'll see you in the firelink at least once a week."

Taryn rolled his eyes. "Okay, Jules. You've said that at least five times since we got up this morning."

"Okay." She smiled, then hesitated. "Well, we'd better go."

After a final hug, Taryn and Julia mounted their steeds and started to ride slowly, giving Johann a moment alone with his youngest son.

"William, I hope you know how grateful I am that I've found you."

"I know. It's just... I..." William struggled with what he was trying to say.

Johann placed his hands on William's shoulders and looked his youngest son in the eye. "It's all right, William. It will take a while, I know." He hugged his son. "I'm looking forward to getting to know you."

William looked at his father and responded from his heart. "I'd like that."

The two men shared a smile and another hug before Johann mounted his steed and rode off to join his two other children. As he rode away, he turned and waved to the young man whose existence he hadn't known of until recently, and who was, and would always be, his son.

Meanwhile, Taryn and Julia had settled in to an easy pace that would allow Johann to catch up with them. During the first few minutes of the ride, each had been lost in thought. Julia, as usual, was the first to share what she had been thinking. "I'm glad we found him, Tay."

"Me too, Jules."

She reached over from where she perched on Firefly's saddle and patted her sibling on the arm. "You'll still be my favorite brother though."

He growled at her half in jest, "I'd better be." Then he looked at her and winked. "And you'll still be my favorite sister."

"Hey. I'm your only sister."

Taryn laughed and mockingly wiped his brow. "Whew. Thank God!"

Julia shot him her best fierce look. It worked about as well as it usually did, which was to say, not at all.

After a few more moments of riding in companionable silence, Julia said, "I hope that we can get to know him and that he'll be a part of our lives."

"I hope so too, but it's up to him."

Just then Skye and Reggie, who had been flying above, chimed in.

Sophie says good-bye and thank you.

Who's Sophie?

211

Julia wondered aloud, "Wasn't that the name of Mother's bird - the one that Father hated?"

Sophie is the name of the gray Dove. William just named her.

Julia looked at her brother and laughed, "Sophie. It's a good name. I don't know how fond of it Father is though."

Just then, Johann rode up and joined them. "Oh no. What is it I'm not fond of, and what are you two up to now?"

"Not us. This one is your other son." Taryn joked good-naturedly.

Johann smiled. That sounded so good to hear. "I can see that in his absence, William will be blamed for a great deal."

Taryn perked up in the saddle. "Great idea! I'll have to remember that one."

Julia shot her brother a look and answered Johann's question. "We were just talking about the name William chose for his gray Dove: Sophie."

"Sophie?" Johann mused for a moment as his two eldest watched for his reaction. "I like it," he said, "and more important, I think your mother would like it, too." He smiled at his children, proud of the people that they had become, so willing to accept a brother they had never known and open their hearts to him.

"I'm proud of you both. You handled this situation with a great deal of courage and compassion."

Taryn and Julia just stared at their normally reticent father. Julia was the first to recover. "Thank you, Father. We did the best we could do. I'm glad you're pleased."

"Then why are you two staring at me?"

This time it was Taryn's turn. "It's just not like you to say things like that."

"You know I'm proud of you and that I love you."

"We know, but you don't usually talk about it."

"Well, things have changed. It's time I shared more of my feelings. You deserve to know how much you mean to me. All of you."

Julia was thoughtful. "I guess a lot of things have changed now. We all have a lot to get used to."

"That's true, but these are good changes."

Taryn decided that they had all had quite enough sentimental discussion for one day. "Hey, Jules..."

She answered him absentmindedly. "Um-hm."

"I know one thing that's never going to change."

"What's that, Tay?"

"You'll always lose to me."

She was slow to come out of her thoughtful state. A bit too slow. "What?"

"Race you to Sarah's," he yelled over his shoulder as he galloped away. "Loser has to kiss Gern."

As always, she rose to the bait. "Ha! You're on! No cheating this time, Tay. Tay. TAY!!!!" She spurred her horse into the familiar action. "C'mon Firefly. Let's show him who the loser is!"

Johann smiled as he watched his two eldest children engage in the friendly competition which was as familiar to them as breathing. He admired the bond that they had, and he was looking forward to watching as they developed a relationship with William. It would be different from their connection, but important all the same. For when it came down to it, Johann knew that family was what this life was all about. It was the only thing that truly mattered.

~~~~~~~~~~~~~~~

As Johann followed behind his children and watched them ride off into the distance, he didn't realize that someone else was watching them as well. High above, riding the continuously shifting air currents, was a large bird of prey. A Falcon.

Suddenly, the bird altered her course and veered away from the siblings she had been following. She didn't need to follow them home. She already knew the way.

Made in the USA
Charleston, SC
16 June 2010